A Fantasy Medley

A Fantasy Medley

EDITED BY YANNI KUZNIA

Subterranean Press 2009

First Edition

ISBN
978-1-59606-224-5

Subterranean Press
PO Box 190106
Burton, MI 48519

www.subterraneanpress.com

TABLE OF CONTENTS

To Brian, for not saying a word
when my pages and books
sprawled through the house.

and

To Amy: the paper is all yours.

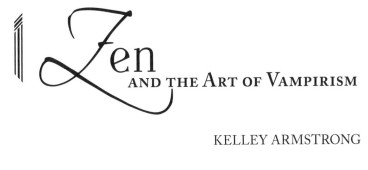

Zen

AND THE ART OF VAMPIRISM

KELLEY ARMSTRONG

In Miller's bar, the only thing that smelled worse than the bathroom was the clientele. Of the three humans there that night, two were already so pissed I could walk over, sink my teeth into their necks, and they'd never flinch. Tempting, but Rudy likes me sticking to beer.

Cultural assimilation is a lofty goal, but every minority needs a place to kick back with her own kind, a place to trade news and gossip that wouldn't interest anyone outside the group. For supernaturals in Toronto, that place is Miller's.

The clientele wasn't exclusively supernatural. That kind of thing is hard to enforce without calling attention to yourself, which none of us wants to do. But the ambiance itself is usually enough to discourage outsiders.

Tonight the only sober human was a guy in a suit sitting at the bar, drinking in his surroundings and telling himself that, despite his house in the suburbs and corporate parking spot, he was still a badass. And as long as he was misbehaving, that Japanese girl in the short skirt and knee-high boots looked like just the thing to cap off his evening. I'd already rejected the two drinks he'd sent, but he wasn't getting the message, not even when I openly eyed the blond half-demon girl at the other end of the bar.

While I'd settle for an introduction to the half-demon, what I really wanted was a job. My rent was due, my bar tab was overdue and if I didn't get a gig in the next week, I'd be digging through my stash of goodies, looking for something to fence. I suppose I could return my new red leather jacket and matching boots. Or not.

A job, though, might be forthcoming. The bartender Rudy said a guy had come by last night, interested in hiring me. I don't usually take jobs without referrals, but desperate times…

I swore I heard the bells of St. James toll midnight when my guy walked in. If that bit of theatrics didn't mark him as a first-timer, the way he entered did—slinking through the door, looking around furtively, hands stuffed in his overcoat pockets like a perv getting ready to flash. The overcoat didn't help. Nor did the rest of the outfit—skin-tight pleather pants, an open-necked shirt and chains. Someone had watched *Underworld* one too many times.

Rudy said the guy had introduced himself as José. If there was an ounce of Hispanic blood in him, I'd drink cow's blood for a week. Probably christened Joe, but decided it wasn't exotic enough for a supernatural.

He made it halfway to the bar before Rudy pointed me out to him. The guy stopped. He looked at me. He looked some more.

Obviously I wasn't what he expected. Unfortunately, he was exactly what I expected—scruffy, stringy hair, wild eyes. Toronto doesn't get a lot of new supernaturals and those who do emigrate are usually on the run from trouble south of the border. I only hoped José didn't want me to fix that trouble for him. I'm a thief, not an assassin, but I've had more than one client imply that it shouldn't make a difference. Vampires kill; therefore, they should have no compunction about doing it for money.

José walked to my table. "Zoe Takano?"

I motioned to the chair across from me.

"It's, uh, about a job," he said.

I motioned at the chair again.

His gaze skittered about the bar. "Shouldn't we, uh, take this outside?"

"Does anyone in here look like an undercover cop?"

He gave a nervous chuckle. "I guess not."

Actually, the hulking half-demon in the corner *was* one, but we had an understanding.

"Tell me what you have in mind," I said. "Just leave out the details until I've agreed."

It was a theft, something about a ring. I didn't pay much attention because after two lines of his story, I knew there was no job. That's when he turned to call a drink order to Rudy, and his hair swung off his neck, revealing the ghosts of a half-dozen puncture wounds.

Vamp freak.

Just as there are humans who get off on bloodletting, there are supernaturals who do, too. The difference is that supernaturals don't need to find someone to play vampire for them. They can get a real one.

In Toronto, there weren't any vamp freaks. There was no point. I was the only vampire here.

I let José natter on, then set my beer aside. "You're right. Let's take this outside."

He jumped up so fast he set the table wobbling. Rudy stood at the bar, scowling, José's drink in hand.

"Pay the man," I said.

José opened his wallet and stared in confusion at the multi-colored bills.

"This one's pretty," I said, plucking out a red fifty. I handed it to Rudy, mouthing for him to apply the extra to my tab. Then I waved José out of the bar.

❦

I led José to an alley two blocks over. He trailed at my heels even when I said he could walk beside me. Someone had him trained well. I shivered and briefly wondered who.

I got far enough down the alley to be hidden from the street, then turned sharply.

"No," I said.

"No?"

"I'm not interested."

"In the job? I thought—"

He stopped as I moved in, getting so close our clothing brushed. Then I lifted onto my tiptoes. I didn't say a word. Just gave him the look. His pupils dilated. His heart raced, the sound of it echoing through the alley, the sight of it pulsing in his neck making my fangs lengthen. He let out a groan and shifted forward, his erection rubbing my leg.

I stepped back. "*That's* what I meant. And the answer is no."

"Please? Just a bite. Just a taste."

I swallowed my revulsion. My fangs retracted. As I took another step back, a crackle sounded behind me. A foot treading on trash.

He kept babbling. "I'm a clean-living Druid. *Totally* clean. No booze. No dope. No cigarettes. I haven't even taken aspirin in months."

"And do you know what all that healthy living is going to get you? A comfy berth in the morgue."

He shook his head. "No, I'm always careful. I know what it feels like when you have to stop. I have a safe word—"

"Which works just fine until it's time for your master's annual kill. That's how it ends, José. That's how it always ends. So take my advice and find a human playmate who'll bite your neck for you and—"

I spun, my kick connecting with the kneecap of a hulking figure behind me. Another spin, another kick—this one to the back of her knee—and she went down.

The woman lying on the ground was at least six-foot-two and well-muscled. A flaxen-haired Amazon. Admittedly, I have a weakness for strong blondes, but I knew drag queens who could pass for female more easily than this woman.

"Brigid Drescher, I presume," I said. "Pleased to meet you."

She snarled, spittle speckling my boots. I bent to wipe it off, then spun fast, fists and foot flying up. The dark-ponytailed vampire sneaking up behind me raised his hands.

"Hey, Hans," I said. "It's been a while."

Forty years, give or take a decade. Last time I saw Hans, he was still going by his real name: John. Now I kicked myself for not figuring out who "owned" José. If his rechristening didn't give it away, his costume should have. Last I heard, Hans was on an Anne Rice kick, but apparently he'd progressed to *Underworld* gear. Either that or he spent his off-hours in a bordello.

As Brigid got to her feet, he turned to her. "I told you there wasn't any use trying to trick Zoe."

Brigid brushed off her leather corset. "I thought you said she didn't fight."

"Only in self-defense. Isn't that right, Zoe?"

I ignored his mocking lilt and managed a perky smile. "You got it. So what brings you two to Toronto?" I had an idea, and hoped I was wrong.

"José," Brigid said before Hans could answer.

She snapped her fingers, and motioned the vamp freak to her side. He pretended not to notice and kept slinking closer to me. I sidestepped. He slunk. Sidestepped. Slunk.

Hans laughed. "I think your boy found something he likes better, Brig. Sorry, José, but you're not Zoe's type. Or gender."

José frowned, taking a moment to get it. Then he smiled and sidled closer.

"Go," I said, flicking my fingers at him. "Shoo."

"José!" Brigid barked.

He slid a look her way, shuddered and wriggled closer to me. Brigid strode over and grabbed him, yelping, by the collar.

"When I tell you to come, you come."

His gaze shunted my way, and Brigid's head shot down to his neck, fangs sinking in. I started to say this wasn't the time for a snack. Then Brigid's head ripped back, a chunk of José's neck in her teeth, arterial blood spurting against the wall. She dropped him and spat out the flesh. José convulsed on the ground, gasping and jerking, hands pressed to his neck, eyes rolling as he tried to stop the flow.

I looked down at him, knowing there was nothing I could do, feeling the old serpent of rage uncoil in my gut. My gaze shot to Brigid but, at the last second, I wrenched it away and turned aside.

"What's the matter, Takano?" Brigid said. "Don't like the sight of blood?"

I counted to five, until the serpent relaxed and slid back into hiding. Then I turned and smiled.

"I have a weak stomach, what can I say?"

José lay on his back now, sightless eyes staring up.

"Well, that was a waste," Hans said, stepping away as the blood seeped toward his boots. "You really need to control your temper, Brig."

"Can we get this conversation over with?" I said. "I'd really rather not be found standing over a dead body." I kept my gaze on Hans, my tone light. "And I do hope you plan to clean this mess up. It's terribly bad form to leave bodies in another vamp's town."

"That's what we're here to talk about," he said. "Your town."

"It's not yours anymore," Brigid said.

That's what I was afraid they were here for. Hans and his little gang had lived in New Orleans. From what I'd heard, they'd been thrilled when Hurricane Katrina hit—a chaos-gripped city makes for easy pickings. But after a year, they'd realized trailer park life really wasn't their style. Since then, they'd been hunting for a new place to settle.

"So you're looking at Toronto?" I laughed. "Seriously? Sure, it's a world-class city, multicultural, blah, blah. But it's *Toronto*. There's a reason a third-rate vamp like me lives here. No one else wants it. Long cold winters. Hot humid summers. Smog so thick you can taste it. Taxes are outrageous, and for what? Free health care? Like we need that."

"You aren't going to give us any trouble, are you, Zoe?"

His voice was smooth and soft, but there was an arrogant tilt to his chin and a condescending twist to his words.

For a moment, I reveled in the visions of what I would have done if he'd said those words a hundred years ago. A vampire's invulnerability makes it difficult to inflict any sensation like pain. But there are ways. And I know them all.

"You're welcome to fight for your territory." Brigid strolled over to stand beside Hans. "But I hear you're a bit of a coward."

"Coward is a strong word."

She walked up until she stood so close I could see a shred of José's skin caught between her teeth. Then she took another step and towered over me.

"Is it?" she said.

I sidestepped to face Hans. "I'll be gone by Friday."

❦

I was born Kioko Takano in 1863. My name meant "happy child" and I fulfilled its promise. My life was unremarkable. I was a cheerful girl with loving parents, who grew into a cheerful young woman with a loving fiancé.

A month before my wedding, a group of missionaries came to our village. One of them was Jane Bowman, a blond English girl not much older than myself. When I met her, I realized why, as dearly as I cared for my fiancé, I could feel no more passion for him than for a brother.

I fell in love with Jane. Madly, desperately in love. She was so vibrant and brilliant and worldly, all the things I was not. I soon learned why she had so much experience for her youth—she was a hundred-year-old vampire. I didn't care. It only made her more exotic and wonderful. I loved her. She loved me. Nothing else mattered.

I ran away with Jane. The next few years were glorious. Then came my twentieth birthday and, for it, she offered me the gift of eternal life. Become a vampire. Be young forever. Be with her forever.

I refused. She wheedled, pleaded, begged. I refused. She called me a coward. I laughed and refused.

❦

Being a gracious hostess, I offered to show Hans and Brigid around Toronto before I left. I'd introduce them to the supernatural community and make the transition easy. For a fee, of course.

We had to wait until after dark. Apparently, Hans was sensitive to daylight. He seemed to think this made him a more authentic vampire. I thought it made him an idiot.

And I wasn't the only one. Rudy got one look at the pair, dressed like they were heading to a BDSM convention, and marched into the back room. He emerged only when I hopped over the bar and helped myself to a beer.

"Not until you pay your tab, Zoe." He plucked the bottle from my hand. "And if you think you're cutting town and not paying? I will hunt you down and rip that pretty little—"

"I'll pay. Just give me a couple weeks to settle into my new place."

Rudy put the beer back and turned to Hans. "You're the new vamps Zoe told me about?"

Hans glanced about us, but it was early and the only patron in Miller's was passed out, probably from the night before.

"Yes," Hans said. "We'll be taking over—"

Rudy slapped a paper onto the bar. "Pay her tab."

Brigid snorted. "We aren't going to—"

"You ever want to set foot in this place again?" Rudy asked.

Hans looked around. "Not particularly."

"You want to take Zoe's place in this city? Be part of the community?"

"We aren't really joiners."

Rudy stuffed the tab into his pocket. "Fine. Just remember, we've got over a hundred sorcerers, witches, half-demons, necromancers and shamans in this city, and the only vampire they've ever known is Zoe. Now, if a *real* vampire comes to town, it's going to make folks nervous—"

"How much?" Hans said.

"Seven-hundred and eighty-two dollars."

Hans pivoted to me. "How much do you drink?"

"One beer a night. It's the paying part that gives me trouble."

"Make it an even grand and you'll get my personal seal of approval," Rudy said.

Hans sighed, pulled a wad of cash from his pocket and peeled off the bills.

As Rudy counted them, he said, "My first piece of advice? Make sure this one—" He pointed at me. "—shows you the ropes."

"That's what I'm doing."

He met my gaze. "*All* of them."

"What do you mean?" Brigid asked.

Rudy looked at her. "Toronto has its peculiarities."

"Like the transit system," I said. "Buses, subways, street cars, high-speed trains to the suburbs." I rolled my eyes. "It's so confusing. Let's go check out the subways now."

I hustled them off, leaving Rudy glaring after me.

❧❦

Back when I'd refused to become a vampire, Jane had invited me to a weekend with her undead friends. To persuade me, she teased. Only there was to be no persuasion. Just a conversion.

Like Jane, most vampires inherit the genes and are reborn on death. There is a second way to become one, but the process is horrific. They say you can't force it on another person. They're wrong.

Months later, when Jane and her friends finished with me, I was half mad. But I was a vampire. She expected me to be grateful. Hadn't she proven how much she loved me, to what lengths she'd go to keep me?

I killed her. As slow and horrible a death as my own conversion. When she was finally gone, I hunted down her friends. Then I slaughtered their human servants and thralls.

※※

Next stop on our Toronto tour: Trinity Church.

As I walked to the front doors, Hans and Brigid stopped short, earning choice words from the stream of shoppers exiting the mall next door.

"What is that?" Brigid said.

"The Church of the Holy Trinity. Pretty, isn't it?"

They stared at me. I reached through the open doors and wiggled my fingers.

"See any smoke yet? I hope not. I really like this jacket."

When they didn't answer, I walked in and waved my arms. A homeless guy circled warily around me.

"We are not going in there," Brigid said.

"Suit yourself."

In the side courtyard, I found a dark-skinned fortyish guy in a gym shirt and sweat pants tending to one of the regulars who refused to set foot in a building. I led Hans and Brigid around to him.

"You need to have that tooth pulled, Frank," Randy was telling the old man, who was dressed in ten layers of clothes despite the warm night. "A dentist *should* do it, but I will if you want."

"What's he doing?" Hans whispered.

"Running a medical clinic for the homeless," I said.

"Why?"

I lifted myself up to his ear. "For the money."

Hans shot me a look.

"Seriously," I said. "Why do you think they wear all those clothes? They're stuffed with cash."

Hans snorted, but Brigid started eyeing the old man.

"I'm kidding," I said, before I was responsible for a wave of homeless deaths.

As the old man tottered away, Randy packed his medical bag.

"Hey, Doc," I said.

"Don't 'hey' me." Randy straightened. "Are these the vamps taking over?"

"Yep. Randall Tolliver, meet—"

"Are they taking over your work for me, too?"

"Um, no, I don't think—"

"What work?" Brigid asked.

"Medical supplies," Randy said. "The clinic can't run without them and we're too underfunded to buy all we need. So Zoe obtains them."

"Steals them," I said.

"How much does that pay?" Brigid asked.

"If I could afford to pay for the theft, I could afford to pay for supplies."

"So it doesn't pay?"

"Sure it does," I chirped. "Huge dividends in self-satisfaction. You'd love it."

They looked at me as if they'd rather swallow a crucifix.

"Well, that's just great," Randy said. "You piss off and leave me in the lurch with, what, two days notice? Thank you, Zoe."

He turned to leave, then slowly pivoted back. "She has warned you about Tee, hasn't she?"

"Tee?" Hans said.

"Tea," I said, taking Hans's arm and leading him away. "Being part of the British Commonwealth, Canadians like their tea. Hot tea, not iced. It takes some getting used to."

"If you don't warn them, Zoe—" Randy called after us.

I coughed to cut him off. "Now, ahead, you'll see the Eaton Centre, one of Toronto's largest shopping malls…"

❦

Hans waited until we were at the mouth of a deserted walkway, then stopped me.

"You really think I'm stupid, don't you?" he said.

I decided it was best not to answer that.

He went on anyway. "I see what you're doing, Zoe, and it's not going to work."

"Doing?"

"First the bartender warns us of some unknown danger in Toronto, then your doctor friend mentions a monster named Tee."

"Monster?" I gave a nervous laugh. "There's no monster."

"Of course there isn't. Really, Zoe, I gave you credit for being a lot more clever than this silly scheme. Do you think Brigid and I are going to be scared off by wild stories? I've been around for two hundred years—too long to be frightened by demons."

"Who said anything about—?" I blurted, then stopped. I stepped back into the shadows and shoved my hands into my pockets. After a moment, I sighed. "I'm sorry. The guys were having some fun with you—playing a prank on the new vamps. I was running interference because I was afraid you'd take it the wrong way."

I adjusted my collar. "I really don't want to cause any trouble."

"Of course you don't," he said smoothly as Brigid rolled her eyes. "That's why we want to make this transition as painless as possible."

"So do I."

"Good. Let's get on with it then."

For my first ten years as a vampire, I never fed and left a living victim. I didn't bother to learn how. And I didn't need to—I found enemies everywhere. If someone so much as shoved me at the market, it would awaken that serpent of rage. I killed and I killed and I killed, and the rage was never sated.

Eventually, I stopped.

There was no dramatic epiphany. No wise vampire showed me a better path. One day I was sitting by a river, caught a glimpse of myself in the water and wished the old myths were true—that vampires cast no reflection. I realized then that the lifetime of a vampire was too long to spend being someone you couldn't bear to see in the mirror.

I moved to the New World and rechristened myself Zoe—a light-hearted, cheerful name. I'd been light-hearted and cheerful once and I vowed I would be again.

And so I reinvented myself. Zoe Takano, cat burglar extraordinaire. The always calm, always cool Zen master of vampirism. Fun, good-natured and easygoing. If you need someone to liven up a party, I'm your girl. To help you in a fight? Not so much.

That's the problem with swearing off the dark stuff. Like an alcoholic, I'm only one good fight away from losing control. It's happened before and it was a long, ugly road to recovery. I can't travel that route again. I might not find my way back.

The next evening, I played realtor, showing Hans and Brigid my apartment.

"It's one of the few units in the building that's still rent-controlled," I said as I led them down the hall. "Being downtown, you get mainly young, single tenants. They come and go so often that I've been here thirty-seven years and no one has noticed I haven't aged a day."

I put my key in the lock.

"And how much would this illegal transfer of tenancy cost us?" Hans asked.

"Three grand, which is an absolute steal. Around here, that wouldn't buy you first and last month's rent for a place like this."

"And that's on top of the thousand I already paid you for playing tour guide?"

"Er, yes, but it's negotiable."

"Seeing as how we've been such good customers," he said dryly.

I faced him. "Whether I leave tomorrow has nothing to do with whether you pay my bar tab or hire my guide services or take over my apartment. I could say you owe me relocation expenses, but we both know I'm not going to challenge you on that. If you don't want to see the apartment, fine. I just thought—"

"Show it to us," he said.

I didn't move.

"Show us the damned apartment," Brigid growled.

When they walked in, I could tell they were impressed. Why wouldn't they be? I'd spent twenty years in Toronto searching for exactly the right place to live, and this apartment was it, with its huge bank of windows taking in a postcard view of the skyline.

They admired the night sky and the panorama of colored lights below, then Hans checked out the apartment itself. Again, it was perfect. Minimalist, but warm and inviting. Every piece had been selected with care, from the leather chairs to the ebony dining set to the priceless artifacts I'd "picked up" over decades of museum heists.

"How much for the whole thing?" Hans asked. "Fully furnished."

Brigid's gaze swept over the apartment, her lip curling. "It's not really my style—"

"It's mine." He met my gaze. "How much?"

"A lot. I don't think you want—"

"I do."

His tone said either I named a price or he'd take it. The serpent uncoiled. I clenched my stomach muscles, sending it back to sleep.

"We'll discuss it," I murmured. "For now, if the location is to your—"

A shuffling rasp came from the bedroom. I went still. But they didn't hear it, only frowned, wondering why I'd stopped.

I put my hands on Hans's back, propelling him toward the door. "Actually, let's discuss this over drinks. My treat. I know this amazing place on Queen's West. Much more your style than Miller's."

He let me push him two feet before locking his knees. "I want this apartment, Zoe."

"Actually, you know, transferring the tenancy might not be that easy…"

The shuffling sound reached the bedroom hall. Brigid heard it now, pivoting that way.

"You want more money?" Hans said. "Is that what this is about? It better not be, because I've dealt fairly with you, and if you screw me over—"

"Mein Gott," Brigid whispered. "What is that?"

Lurching from the bedroom hall was a woman. I already knew her gender—otherwise, it would be impossible to tell. Gauzy rags encased her skeletal limbs. A tangled mass of matted white hair hid her face. As she shuffled forward, her bony fingers waved in front of her as if she was conducting an orchestra no one else could see. Her head bobbed, sunken eyes glittering with madness, fleshless lips moving soundlessly.

Seeing me, the woman stopped. She squinted, head weaving like a hawk trying to get a better look at its prey.

"Tee," I said, "W-what are you doing here? How'd you get—?"

"Going somewhere, Zoe?"

I bit off a nervous laugh. "Uh, no. Of course not."

"That's not what Tee heard. She heard you're leaving us. Running off because big bad vampires have come to town again." She looked at Brigid and Hans and sniffed. "Are these them? Nasty creatures."

"Hey!" Brigid stepped toward Tee, then thought better of it and stopped, crossing her arms over her chest. "Whatever that monster is—"

"Monster?"

Tee unfurled her limbs, pulling herself up until she was almost as tall as Brigid. She shuffled toward her, rags whispering against the hardwood floor. Brigid tried holding her ground, but when she caught a whiff of Tee, she drew back.

"A monster kills and does not feed," Tee said. "A monster leaves pretty boys to die in ugly alleys."

"José?" Hans said. "That was—"

"There was another, last night. The one this naughty vampire didn't tell you about." She drew herself up again to look Brigid in the eye. "The pretty boy with the pretty red hair and the pretty red shirt and all that pretty red blood."

"How did you—?" Brigid began.

"Tee knows everything. Her friends tell her."

Tee swept a hand around the room. Brigid and Hans followed it, but saw nothing.

I stepped forward. "And that is the great thing about you, isn't it, Tee? You have a regular army of spirit informants."

Tee rocked back on her heels, lips smacking in self-satisfaction. "Tee and her friends help little Zoe."

"Exactly, and now you can help Hans and Brigid."

Her lips pursed and she eyed them. "One vampire is enough for any city." She sidled toward Hans and whispered. "Give Tee the naughty one, and she won't ask for morsels for a very long time."

"Morsels?" Hans's gaze shot to me.

"Er, yes. See…"

I motioned him off to the side. When Tee tried to follow, I waved her away. She grumbled, then stumped over to a chair.

"Tee's a demon," I said, voice lowered. "She got trapped in a human body a hundred years ago. Being a demon, she can't die, which is why she…looks like that. But over the years, she's misplaced a few of her marbles."

"A few?"

"Most of the bag. Anyway, she's convinced that she's alive because she's found the key to immortality: consuming the flesh of the living."

"What?"

I motioned for him to keep his voice down. "Usually she just takes a few nibbles off dead bodies. Sometimes she does hunt—"

"Tee eats what she hunts," she called. "Not like some people." She glowered at Brigid.

I lowered my voice another notch. "We discourage the hunting. It's messy. Instead, Tee and I have an arrangement. Her spirit friends help me and I feed her."

"Feed her what?"

"If you're looking for immortality, what's better than the flesh of the living?"

Hans stared at me. He blinked. Then he eased back with a harsh laugh. "If you really expect me to believe that you feed her—"

I took a penknife from my pocket, sliced a strip of flesh from the underside of my forearm, then walked over and gave it to Tee. She gobbled it down like a strip of bacon.

Behind me, the room went silent. I flexed my arm. The flesh was already filling in the furrow.

"So." I smiled brightly. "That's all there is to it. Now, let's get that drink and we can talk terms. There are a few pieces here I couldn't bear to part with, but the rest is negotiable."

I walked to the door. Hans and Brigid didn't move.

"We don't like them," Tee muttered. "We don't like them at all. Nasty things. We like Zoe."

I sighed. "Yes, it'll be an adjustment, Tee, but you'll get used to them." Another bright smile. "I'm sure we all taste the same."

"Okay," Brigid said, hands flying up. "That's it. Zoe might put up with your shit, demon, but I won't. If you ever try to take a bite of me—"

Brigid sailed off her feet, smacked into the wall and collapsed at the bottom.

"She's a demon, remember?" I whispered. "You don't say no to a demon."

"The hell I don't," Brigid snarled.

She leaped up...and got hit in the gut with an energy bolt. The smell of burning flesh filled the room. Tee hadn't budged, just sat placidly stroking the leather chair.

"We don't like her." Tee looked at Hans. "We don't like you, either, but we like her less. Give her to Tee. Tee has a good hiding place, dark and cold. She'll save all the naughty vampire's bits and eat them slowly."

Brigid let out a growl, pawing the ground like a bull.

I swung over to Tee and squeezed her shoulder. "Ah, Tee, you're such a joker. You'd never do that, would you? Not to a big, strong vampire like Brigid."

"Even vampires sleep," Tee murmured. "Yes, they do." Her gaze darted around, listening to her spirit counsel. "That's how we'll do it. We'll get her when—"

"Tee," I said sharply.

She pouted and grumbled under her breath.

"I'm not staying in the same city as that thing," Brigid said. "Either she goes or I do."

Tee launched herself at Brigid. The vampire stumbled back, arms sailing up to ward her off. Then she stiffened and fell over.

"Shit!" I said. "Her binding powers. Hans, grab her before—"

Too late. Tee was on Brigid, biting chunks of flesh from her shoulder. Hans and I managed to get her off. I restrained her, thrashing and howling, as the binding spell broke and Brigid scrambled to her feet. As they ran for the door, I dropped Tee and tore after them.

"Wait! We had a deal! I'll give you a discount on the apartment—"

I caught up with them in the stairwell. We had a brief discussion, the upshot being that I could keep my damned city and they were never setting foot in this godforsaken town again. I begged. I pleaded. I cajoled. All to no avail.

I walked back into my apartment. Rudy and Randy were helping themselves to my bar.

"That went well," I said. "Thanks for the spells, guys."

Rudy and Randy were half-brothers. With different mothers and twenty years between them, they didn't look much alike. The only thing they shared was their father's sorcerer blood.

Tee was back in her chair, now stroking a Maori mask she'd plucked from the shelf. She whispered under her breath. Talking to her spirits. Tee wasn't a demon—just a very old, very powerful, very crazy necromancer terrified of death, certain it would condemn her to an eternity of serving ghosts.

I cut another strip from my arm and handed it to her. She gobbled it down. Randy turned away; Rudy glowered at me.

"It grows back," I said. "And it's better than having her hunt humans."

"Well, don't do it while I'm here, okay?" Rudy helped himself to my daiginjô-shu.

"That'll be twenty bucks," I said. "You can add it to my credit."

"Credit?"

"You got a grand for a fifty-dollar tab, most of which José already paid off. I expect at least five-hundred in credit."

"Sure, we could do that." He headed for the couch, circling wide around Tee. "Or I could introduce you to the blond half-demon. She asked about you last night. Of course, not having any experience with vampires, she's a little nervous about introducing herself..."

"Keep the money."

He sat. "I'm sure you had fun with this scheme, but you could have saved yourself a lot of trouble and just killed them."

"Me?"

He gave me a look that said I didn't fool him. I never had.

Randy handed Tee a glass of my cheaper sake. She whispered under her breath and petted his hand before he continued on to the sofa.

"Normally, I'd be all for the humane solution," Randy said. "But in this case, killing them might have *been* the humane solution. At least for everyone else."

True. I did the world no favors by sparing Brigid's life. I could argue that in killing her, I could unleash a worse predator inside me. But that's bullshit rationalization. I let her live because I wouldn't risk the personal hell that could come with killing her.

I have a good life here. A damned near perfect one. Would I kill to keep it? I'd rather not find out. Someday, I'll be tested. Just not today.

I pulled out the watch I'd swiped from Hans when we were struggling with Tee.

"Anyone want a Rolex?"

Riding
THE SHORE OF THE RIVER
OF DEATH

KATE ELLIOTT

This wooded western country far from their tribal lands in the east smelled raw and unpalatable to Kereka, but the hawk that circled overhead had the same look as hawks in the grasslands. Some things were the same no matter where you went, even if you had to ride into the lands where foreigners made their homes to get what you wanted. Even if you had to journey far from your father's authority and your mother's tent to seize the glory of your first kill.

The reverberant thunk of an axe striking wood surprised her; she'd thought it was too early to hunt because they had yet to see any sign of habitation. Ahead, barely visible within the stretch of pine and beech through which they rode, her brother Belek unslipped his spear from its brace against his boot and urged his mare into a run. Kereka rose in her stirrups to watch him vanish into a clearing occluded by summer's leaves. Birds broke from cover, wings flashing. The clatter of weapons, a sharp shriek, and then a man's howl of pain chased off through the bright woodland.

Edek, riding in front of her, whipped his horse forward. His voice raised in a furious burst of words as he and Kereka broke out of the woods and into a clearing of grass, meadow flowers, bold green saplings, and a pair of sturdy young oak trees.

Belek's mare had lost her rider. She shied sideways and stood with head lifted and ears flat. Beside the oaks, two had fought. Belek's spear had thrust true, skewering the foreign man through the torso, but the farmer's axe had cut into the flesh below Belek's ribs before Belek had finally killed the man with a sword-thrust up under the ribs. Edek stood with mouth working soundlessly, watching as Belek sawed off the head of the dead man with his bloodied knife. Blood leaked from Belek's gut, trailing from under his long felt tunic and over the knees of his leather trousers, but he was determined to get that head.

If he could present the head to the *begh* before he died, then he would die as a man rather than a boy.

His teeth were gritted and his eyes narrowed, but he uttered no word that might betray how much he hurt. Even when he got the head detached so it rolled away from the body, blood spilling brightly onto the grass, he said nothing, only uttered a 'gah' of pain as he toppled over to one side. His left hand clutched the hair of the dead man. With his gaze he tracked the sky, skipping from cloud to cloud, and fetched up on Kereka's face. He seemed about to speak but instead passed out.

Kereka stared. One of the young oaks had a gash in its side, but the farmer hadn't chopped deep enough to fell it. Bugs crawled among the chips of wood cut from the trunk. A cluster of white flowers had been crushed by the farmer's boots. His red blood mingled with Belek's, soaking into the grass. This could not be happening, could it?

Every year boys rode out of the clans to seek their first kill, and every year some did not return. Riding the shore of the river of death was the risk you took to become a man. Yet no lad rode out in the dawn's thunder thinking death would capture *him*.

Edek dismounted and knelt beside Belek to untie the heavy tunic, opening it as one might unfold the wings of a downed bird. Seeing the deep axe cut and the white flash of exposed rib, he swore softly. Kereka could not find words as she absorbed the death of her hopes.

"He'll never get home with this wound," said Edek. "We'll have to leave him." He started, hearing a crack, but it was only Belek's mare stepping on a fallen branch as it turned to move back toward the familiarity of its herd.

"We can't leave him." Kereka knew she had to speak quickly before she succumbed to the lure of Edek's selfish suggestion. "He is my brother. The *begh*'s son. It will bring shame on us if we abandon him."

Edek shrugged. "If we take him back, then you and I have no chance of taking a head. You must see that. He can't ride. He's dead anyway. Let's leave him and ride on. Others have done it."

She set her jaw against his tempting words. "Other boys who were left to die hadn't already taken a head. He's taken his head, so we must give him a chance to die as a man. We'll lose all honor if we leave him. Even if both of us took a head in our turn."

"I don't want to wait another season. I'm tired of being treated as a boy when I'm old enough to be a man."

"Go on alone if you wish, Edek the whiner." Kereka forced out the mocking words, and Edek's sullen frown deepened with anger. "You'll sour the milk with your curdling tongue. You can suckle on your grievances for another season. You'll get another chance to raid."

As she would not.

Last moon the *begh*'s son from the Pechanek clan had delivered six mares to her father, with the promise of twenty sheep, ten fleeces, two bronze cauldrons, a gilded saddle, three gold-embroidered saddle blankets, five felt rugs, and a chest of gold necklaces and bronze belt clasps as her bride price. Her father's wives and the mothers of the tribe had been impressed by the offer. They had been charmed by Prince Vayek's respectful manners and pleasing speeches. Perhaps most of all they had been dazzled by his handsome face and well proportioned body displayed to good effect in several bouts of wrestling, all of which he had won against the best wrestlers of the Kirshat clan. Her father and uncles had praised his reputation as a mighty warrior, scourge of the Uzay and Torkay clans, and all the while their gazes had returned again and again to the deadly iron gleam of the griffin feathers he wore as his warrior's wings. Other warriors, even other *beghs* and their princely sons, wore ordinary wings, feathers fastened with wire to wooden frames that were riveted to an armored coat. Only a man who had slain a griffin could fly griffin wings. Such a man must be called a hero among men, celebrated, praised, and admired.

Her father had decreed she would wed Prince Vayek at the next full moon. Wed, and be marked as a woman forever, even unto death.

This was her last chance to prove her manhood.

When she spoke, her voice was as harsh as a crow's. "We'll weave a litter of sticks and drag him behind his horse."

Dismounting, she turned her back so Edek could not see her wipe away the hot tears. Honor did not allow her to cry. She wanted to be a man and live a man's life, not a woman's. But she could not abandon her dying brother.

⚒

Grass flattened under the weight of a litter as Belek's mare labored up a long slope. Kereka rode at a walk just in front of Belek's horse, its lead tied to her saddle. Her own mare, summer coat shiny in the hot sun, flicked an ear at a fly.

She glanced back at the land falling away to the west. She had lagged behind to shoot grouse in the brush that cloaked a stream, its banks marked at this distance by the crowd of trees and bushes flourishing alongside running water. She squinted into the westering sun, scanning the land for pursuers, but saw no movement. Yesterday they had left the broken woodland country behind. Out here under the unfenced sky, they'd flown beyond the range of the farmers and their stinking fields.

From ahead, Edek called her name. She whistled piercingly to let him know she was coming. The two birds she'd killed dangled from a line hooked to the saddle of Belek's horse. Belek himself lay strapped to the litter they had woven of sapling branches. He had drifted in and out of consciousness for four days. It was amazing he was still alive, but he had swallowed drips and drops of mare's blood, enough to keep breath in his body. Now, however, his own blood frothed at his lips. The end would come soon.

Maybe if he died now, before they reached the tents of the Kirshat clan, she and Edek could turn immediately around, ride back west, and take up their hunt in fresh territory. Yet even to think this brought shame; Belek deserved to die as a man, whatever it meant to her.

She topped the rise to see hills rolling all the way to the eastern horizon. Dropping smoothly away from her horse's hooves lay a long grassy hollow half in shadow with the late afternoon light. The ground bellied up again beyond the hollow like a pregnant woman's distended abdomen. Edek had dismounted partway up the farther slope. He'd stripped out of his tunic in the heat and crouched with the sun on his back as he examined the ground. Above him, thick blocks of stone stood like sentries at the height of the hill: a stone circle, dark and forbidding.

The sight of the heavy stones made her ears tingle, as though someone was trying to whisper a warning but couldn't speak loudly enough for her to hear. A hiss of fear escaped her, and at once she spat to avert spirits who might have heard that hiss and seek to capture her fear and use it against her. She whistled again, but Edek did not look up. With its reins dropped over its head, his mount grazed in a slow munch up the slope toward the looming stones. He had his dagger out and was digging at the dirt. His quiver shifted on his bare back as he hunkered forward. What was he doing, leaving himself vulnerable like that?

She nudged her mare forward. When the reins tightened and pulled, Belek's mare braced stubbornly, then gave in and followed. The litter bumped over a rough patch of ground. Belek grunted, whimpered. Eyes fluttering, he muttered spirit words forced out of him where he lay spinning between the living world and the world of the spirits. A bubble of blood swelled and popped on his lips. The head of the farmer he had slain bumped at his thigh. Its lank hair tangled in his fingers. The skin had gone gray, and it stank.

Edek did not look up when she halted behind him. She touched the hilt of the sword slung across her back. Once they reached the tribe, she would have to give it back to her uncle. Only men carried swords.

"What if I had been your enemy?" she asked. She drew the sword in a swift, practiced slide and lowered its tip to brush Edek between the shoulder blades.

He did not look up or even respond. He was trying to pry something out of the densely packed soil. The sun warmed his back as he strained. As the quiver shifted with each of his movements, the old Festival scars on his back pulled and retracted, displaying the breadth of his back to great advantage. She didn't like Edek much; he was good-looking enough to expect girls to admire him, but his family wasn't wealthy enough that he could marry where he pleased, and that had made him bitter, so in a way she understood his sulks and frowns. And she could still ogle his back, sweating and slick under the sun's weight.

Suddenly he hooked his dagger under an object and with a grunt freed it from an entangling root and the weight of moist soil. When he flipped it into plain view, she sucked in breath between teeth in astonishment.

The sun flashed in their eyes and she threw up a hand to shield herself from the flare. Edek cried out. From Belek came a horrible shriek more like the rasp of a knife on stone than a human cry. Only the horses seemed unmoved.

She lowered her hand cautiously. At first glance, the object seemed nothing more than an earth-encrusted feather, but as Edek cautiously wiped the vanes with the sleeve of his tunic, the cloth separated as though sliced. Where dirt flaked away, the feather glinted with a metallic sheen unlike that of any bird's feather.

"It's a griffin's feather!" said Edek.

Kereka was too amazed and humbled to speak, awed by its solidity, its beauty, its strength. Its sacred, powerful magic. Only shamans and heroes possessed griffin feathers.

He shifted in his crouch to measure her, eyes narrowed. "Even a humble clansman can aspire to wed a *begh*'s daughter if he brings a griffin's feather as her bride price."

Kereka snorted. "Even one you dug up from the dirt?"

"The gods give gifts to those they favor!"

"You'll set yourself against the mighty Vayek and the entire Pechanek clan? Who will listen to your bleating, even with a griffin feather in your hand to dazzle their eyes?"

"Who will listen? Maybe the one who matters most." How he stared! He'd never been so bold before! She shook a hand in annoyance, like swatting away a fly, and he flushed, mouth twisting downward.

The feather's glamour faded as the shadow of afternoon crept over their position. And yet, at the height of the hill to the east, a glimmer still brightened the air.

How could they see the setting sun's flash when they were facing east, not west?

"Look!" she cried.

A woman stood framed and gleaming within the western portal of stone and lintel. Sparks flowered above the stones in a pattern like the unfurling of wings sewn out of gold, the fading banner of a phoenix. So brief its passage; the last embers floating in the air snapped, winked bright, and vanished.

Edek stared, mouth agape.

The woman, not so very far away, watched them. She had black hair, bound into braids but uncovered, and a brown face and dark hands. She wore sandals bound by straps that wound up her calves over tight leggings suitable for riding. A close-fitting bodice of supple leather was laced over a white shirt. But she wore no decent skirts or heavy knee length tunic or long robe; her legs were gloved in cloth, but she might as well have been bare, for you could imagine her shape quite easily. She wore no other clothing at all unless one could count as clothing her wealth of necklaces. Made of gold and beads, they draped thickly around her shoulders like a collar of bright armor.

A woman of the Quman people who displayed herself so brazenly would have been staked down and had the cattle herd driven across her to obliterate her shame. But this woman seemed unaware of her own nakedness. Edek could not stop staring at that shapely bodice and those form-fitting trousers even as the woman hefted her spear and regarded them with no sign of fear.

"Chsst!" hissed Edek, warding himself with a gesture. "A witch!"

"A witch, maybe, but armed with stone like a savage," muttered Kereka in disgust. Anyway, even a woman who carried a spear was of no use to her.

A shape moved behind the foreigner: broad shoulders, long hair, sharp nose. Of course no woman would be traveling alone! Edek did not see the man because he was blinded by lust. Let him hesitate, and she would take the prize. This was her chance to take a head and never have to marry the Pechanek *begh*'s son.

Kereka sliced the halter rope that bound Belek's horse to her saddle, and drove her mare up the hill. A Quman warrior rode in silence, for he had wings to sing the song of battle for him. She had no wings yet—only men were allowed to wear armor and thereby fly the honored pennant of warrior's wings—but she clamped her lips tight down over a woman's trilling ululation, the goad to victory. She would ride in silence, like a man.

The horse was surefooted and the hill none too steep. Edek had only a moment in which to cry out an unheeded question before he scrambled for his mount. Ahead, the woman retreated behind one of the huge stones. The man had vanished. Kereka grinned, yanked her mare to the right, and swung round to enter the stone circle at a different angle so she could flank them.

"*Sister! Beware!*"

The words rasped at the edge of her hearing.

It was too late.

She hit the trap with all the force of her mare's weight and her own fierce desire for a different life than the one that awaited her. A sheet of pebbles spun under its hooves. A taut line of rope took her at the neck, and she went tumbling. She hit the ground so hard, head cracking against stone, that she could not move. The present world faded until she could see, beyond it, into the shimmering lights of the spirit world where untethered souls wept and whispered and danced. Belek reached out to her, his hand as insubstantial as the fog that swallows the valleys yet never truly possesses them. It was his spirit voice she heard, because he was strong enough in magic for his spirit to bridge the gap.

"*Sister! Take my hand!*"

"I will not go with you to the other side!" she cried, although no sound left her mouth. In the spirit world, only shamans and animals could speak out loud. "But I will drag you back here if it takes all my strength!"

She grasped his hand and *tugged*. A fire as fierce as the gods' anger rose up to greet her. She had to shield her eyes from its heat and searing power. She blinked back tears as the present world came into focus again.

It was night. Twilight had passed in what seemed to her only an instant while she had swum out of the spirit world.

Pebbles ground uncomfortably into her buttocks. A stalk of grass tickled the underside of one wrist. Tiny feet tracked on her forehead, then vanished as the creature flew. She sat propped against the rough wall of a standing stones, wrists and ankles bound. How had this happened? She could not remember.

The scene before her lay in sullen colorless tones, lit by a grazing moon and by the blazing stars. Each point of light marked a burning arrow shot into the heavens by the warrior Tarkan, he who had bred with a female griffin and fathered the Quman people.

The flaring light of a campfire stung her eyes. The man crouched before it, raking red coals to one side. He had a thick beard, like the northern farmers, and skin pale enough that it was easy to follow his gestures as he efficiently scalded and plucked *her grouse* and roasted them over coals. Grease dripped and sizzled, the smell so sweet it was an insult thrown in her face.

Where were the others?

Edek lay well out of her reach, slumped against one of the giant stones. The horses stood hobbled just beyond the nimbus of light; she saw them only as shapes. Belek's litter lay at the edge of the harsh and restless flare of the fire. Still strapped to the litter, he moaned and shuddered. The woman appeared out of the darkness as abruptly as a shaman's evil dream. She crouched beside him with both hands extended. Lips moving but without sound, she sprinkled grains of dirt or flakes of herbs over his body.

Fear came on Kereka in the same way a spirit sickness does, penetrating the eyes first and sinking down to lodge in the throat and, at last, to grasp hold of her belly like an ailment. There are ways to animate dead flesh with sorcery. She had to stop the working, or Belek would be trapped by this creature's magic and never able to find his way past the spirit-lands to the ancient home of First Grandfather along the path lit by Tarkan's flaming arrows. But she could not move, not even to push her foot along the ground to kick the corpse and dislodge Belek's spirit.

Mist and darkness writhed between dying youth and foreign woman. With a powerful inhalation, the woman sucked in the cloud. Belek thrashed as foam speckled his lips. The witch rocked forward to balance so lightly on her toes that Kereka was sure she would fall forward onto Belek's unprotected chest. Instead, the woman exhaled, her breath loud in the silence; the air glittered with sparks expelled from her mouth. They dissolved into the youth's flesh as the witch settled smoothly back on her heels. She lifted her gaze to look directly at Kereka.

No matter how vulnerable she appeared, indecently clothed and armed only with a stone-pointed spear in the midst of the grasslands, she had power. As the *begh* Bulkezu, ancestor of Kereka's ancestors, had wrapped himself in an impenetrable coat of armor in his triumphant war against the westerners, this woman was armed with something more dangerous than a physical weapon. She was not the bearded man's wife or slave, but his master.

She nodded to mark Kereka's gaze, and spoke curtly in a language unlike any of those muttered by the tribe's slaves.

Kereka shook her head, understanding nothing. It would be better to kill the witch, but in the event, she had no choice except to negotiate from a position of weakness. "What do you want from us? My father will pay a ransom—"

As if her voice awakened him, Belek murmured as in a daze. "Kereka? Are you there?" Rope creaked as he fought with unexpected strength against his bonds. He looked up at the woman crouched above him. "Who are you? Where is my sister—?"

The witch rose easily to her feet and moved away into the gloom. The bearded man stood up and followed her. Kereka heard them speaking, voices trading back and forth in the manner of equals, not master and slave. Two warriors might converse in such tones, debating the best direction for a good hunt, or two female cousins or friendly co-wives unravel an obstacle tangling the weave of family life within their tents.

Belek tried again, voice spiking as he tried to control his fear. "Kereka? Edek?"

"Chsst!" Kereka spoke in a calming voice. She adored her brother, son of her father's third wife, but he was the kind of person who felt each least pebble beneath him when he slept, and although he never complained—what Quman child would and not get beaten for being weak?—he would shift and scoot and brush at the ground all night to get comfortable and thus disturb any who slept next to him. "We're here, Belek. We had to tie you down to keep you on the litter. You'd taken a wound. Now, we have been captured by foreigners."

"I feel a sting in my gut. Ah. Aah!" He grunted, bit back a curse, thapped his head against the litter, and yelped. These healthy noises, evidence of his return from the threshold of the spirit world, sang in her belly with joy. "I remember when I charged that dirty farmer, but nothing after it. Did I get his head?"

"Yes. We tied it to your belt."

His hand groped; he found the greasy hair. "Tarkan's blessings! But what happened to me?"

He deserved to know the worst. "The woman is a witch. She trapped us with sorcery. I think she must have healed you."

"Aie! Better dead than in her debt! If it's true, I am bound to her and she can take from me whatever she wants in payment."

His fretful tone irritated her. "No sense panicking! Best we get free of her, then."

"It's not so simple! The binding which heals has its roots in the spirit world and can't be so easily escaped. Her magic can follow me wherever I go—"

"Then it's best we get back to the tribe quickly and ask for the shamans to intercede. There's a knife at your belt. You should be able to cut yourself loose."

Obedient as always to her suggestions, he writhed under the confining ropes. "Eh! Fah! Knife's gone."

Night lay everywhere over them. The fattening moon grazed on its dark pastures. Kereka clenched her teeth in frustration. There must be some way to free themselves!

Only then did she see a stockpile of weapons—*their* good Kirshat steel swords, iron-pointed arrows, and iron-tipped spears—heaped beyond the campfire, barely visible in the darkness. A stubborn gleam betrayed the griffin's feather, resting atop the loot in the seat of honor.

The foreigners ceased speaking and walked back into the fire's aura. The witch still carried her primitive spear and she was now brandishing a knife that gleamed in black splendor, an ugly gash of obsidian chipped away to make one sharp edge. She had not even bothered to arm herself with the better weapons she had captured, although the bearded man wore a decent iron sword at his side, foreign in its heft and length.

The woman crouched again beside Belek.

Anything was better than pleading—that was a woman's duty, not a man's—but the knife's evil gleam woke such fear in Kereka's heart that she knew such distinctions no longer mattered.

"I beg you, listen to my words. Belek is the honored son of the Kirshat *begh*'s third wife. He has powerful magic. The shamans have said so. He has already entered the first tent of apprenticeship. To kill him would be to release his anger and his untrained power into the spirit world. You don't want that!"

Where there is no understanding there can be no response. And yet, the woman weighed her sorcerer's knife and, with a flicker of a smile, sheathed it. Instead, she slid a finger's length needle of bone from a pouch slung from her belt.

Leather cord bit into Kereka's skin, tightening as she wiggled her hands and only easing its bite when she stilled. She could do nothing to spare Belek whatever torture this creature meant to inflict on him. Witchcraft had bound her to the rock.

The woman caught hold of her own tongue. With exaggerated care she slid the fine needle point through thick pink flesh. Then, with a delicacy made more horrifying for the sight of her bland expression in the face of self mutilation, she slid the needle back out of her tongue, leaned over Belek, and let those drops of blood mingle with the drying froth on Belek's lips.

He struggled, but he too was bound tight. He gasped, swallowed, grimaced; then he sighed as if his breath had been pulled out of him, and abruptly his head lolled back. He had fainted. Or been murdered.

"Tarkan's curse on you!" Kereka shouted. "I'll have my revenge in my brother's name and in the name of the Kirshat tribe! Our father will drive his warband against you even to the ends of the earth—"

The woman laughed, and Kereka sputtered to a halt, her mouth suddenly too dry to moisten words. The skin on her neck crawled as with warning of a storm about to blow down over the grass.

The witch gestured, and the bearded man came forward, knelt beside Belek, and dribbled water from a pouch into his mouth. Belek sputtered, choked, spat, eyes blinking furiously. The bearded man stoppered the pouch and dragged the litter over to rest in the lee of the great stone to Kereka's right. He offered water to Kereka, wordlessly, and she tipped back her head to let the cool liquid flow down her parched throat. She knew better than to refuse it. She needed time to think about that knowing laugh.

He returned to the fire. Tearing apart the grouse, he ate one, wrapped the rest of the meat in a woven grass mat, then curled up on the ground beneath a cloak. The woman settled down cross-legged to stare into the fire. Occasionally she fed it with dried pats of dung.

Night passed, sluggish and sleepy. Kereka dozed, woke, tried to worm her way out of her bonds but could not. No matter how hard she tried to roll away from the monolith, she could not separate herself from the stone. She hissed to get Belek's attention, saw his eyes roll and his mouth work, but no sound emerged except for a faint wordless groan.

The witch woman did not stir from her silent contemplation of the campfire. Now and again a bead of blood leaked from between her lips, and each time as it pearled on her lips she licked it away as if loathe to let even that droplet escape her. She did not speak to them, did not test the bonds that held them, only waited, tasting nothing except her own blood.

❦

Very late a sword moon, thin and curved, rose out of the east. Soon after, the light changed, darkness lightening to gray and at last ceding victory to the pinkish tint of dawn.

The woman roused. Picking up the pouch, she trickled water into Belek's mouth; he gulped, obviously awake, but still he said nothing. She approached Kereka.

As she leaned in to offer water, Kereka caught the scent of her, like hot sand and bitter root. She tried to grab at her with her teeth, any way of fighting back, but the woman jumped nimbly back and grinned mockingly. The man chuckled and spoke words in their harsh foreign tongue as he flung off the cloak and stretched to warm his muscles.

The brilliant disc of the sun nosed above the horizon to paint the world in daylight colors.

From the bundle of gear heaped by a stone, the bearded man unearthed a shovel and set to work digging a shallow ditch just outside the limit of the stones. It was hard work, even though he was only scraping away enough of the carpet of grass and its dense tangle of roots to reveal the black earth. The woman joined him, taking a turn. The grasslands were tough, like its people, unwilling to yield up even this much. Both soon stripped down to shirt and trousers, their shirts sticking to their backs, wet through with sweat. It was slave's work, yet they tossed words back and forth in the manner of free men. And although the woman's form was strikingly revealed, breasts outlined by the shirt's fabric, nipples erect from the effort and heat, the bearded man never stared at her as men stared at women whose bodies they wanted to conquer. He just talked, and she replied, and they passed the shovel back and forth, sharing the work as the ditch steadily grew from a scar, to a curve, to a half-circle around the stones.

Kereka waited until they had moved out of sight behind her. "Hsst! Belek? Edek?"

Yet when there came no answer, she was afraid to speak louder lest she be overheard.

The sun crept up off the eastern horizon as the foreigners toiled. Shadows shortened and shifted; the sloping land came clear as light swallowed the last hollows of darkness. It was a cloudless day, a scalding blue that hurt the eye. Kereka measured the sun's slow rise between squinted eyes: two hands; four hands. A pair of vultures circled overhead but did not land. The steady scrape of the shovel and the spatter of clumps of dirt sprayed on the ground serenaded her, moving on from behind her and around to her right, closing the circle.

The sound caught her ear first as a faint discordance beneath the noise of digging. She had heard this precious and familiar music all her life, marked it as eagerly as the ring of bells on the sheep she was set to watch as a little girl or the scuff of bare feet spinning in the dances of Festival time.

The wind sings with the breath of battle, the flight of the winged riders, the warriors of the Quman people. It whistles like the approach of griffins whose feathers, grown out of the metals of the earth, thrum their high calls in the air.

Kereka scrambled to get her feet under her, shoved up along the rough surface of the stone. She had to see, even if she couldn't escape the stone's grip. Their enemies heard Quman warriors before they saw them, and some stood in wonder, not knowing what that whirring presaged, while others froze in fear, knowing they could not run fast enough to outpace galloping horses.

Belek struggled against the ropes that bound him but gained nothing. Edek neither moved nor spoke.

The woman and bearded man had worked almost all the way around the stones. The woman spoke. The man stopped digging. They stood in profile, listening. She shook her head, and together, shoulders tense, they trotted back into the stones straight to Edek's limp body. The bearded man grabbed the lad by his ankles and dragged him down to the scar. The body lay tumbled there; impossible to say if he was breathing. The woman gestured peremptorily, and the bearded man leaped away from the bare earth and ran up to the nearest stone, leaning on the haft of the shovel, panting from the exertion as he watched her through narrowed eyes.

The obsidian blade flashed in the sun. She bent, grabbed Edek's hair, and tugged his head back to expose his throat. With a single cut she sliced deep.

Kereka yelped. Did the witch mean to take Edek's head as a trophy, as Quman lads must take a head to prove themselves as men?

Belek coughed, chin lifting, feet and hands twitching as he fought against his bonds. He could see everything but do nothing.

Blood pumped sluggishly from Edek's throat. The witch grabbed him by the ankles and, with his face in the dirt and his life's blood spilling onto the black earth, dragged him along the scar away around the circle. All the while her lips moved although Kereka heard no words.

The bearded man wiped his mustache and nose with the back of a grimy hand, shrugged his shoulders to loosen the strain of digging, and dropped the shovel beside their gear. With the casual grace of a man accustomed to fighting, he pulled on a quilted coat and over it a leather coat reinforced with overlapping metal plates. He set out two black crossbows, levering each back to hook the trigger and ready a bolt. After, he drew on gloves and strapped on a helm before gathering up a bow as tall as he was, a quiver of arrows, an axe, and his sword and trotting away out of Kereka's line of sight, again carrying the shovel.

The woman appeared at the other limit of the scar, still towing Edek's body. Where they had ceased digging, a gap opened, about five paces wide. He gestured with the shovel. She shook her head, with a lift of her chin seeming to indicate the now-obvious singing of wings. The two argued, a quick and brutal exchange silenced by two emphatic words she spat out. She arranged the body to block as much of the gap as possible. With a resigned shrug, the bearded man took up a defensive position behind one of the stones to line up on the gap.

Brushing her hands off on her trousers, the witch jogged over to the gear, hooked a quiver of bolts onto her belt, and picked up both crossbows. Women did not wear armor, of course; Kereka knew better than to expect that even this remarkable creature would ever have been fitted with a man's accoutrements. Yet when she sauntered to take a measure of cover behind the standing stone nearest the gap, her easy pace, her lack of any outward sign of nervousness, made her seem far more powerful than her companion, who was forced to rely on leather and metal to protect himself. She propped one crossbow against the stone and, holding the other, straightened. The sun illuminated her haughty face. As she surveyed the eastern landscape and the golden hills, she smiled, a half twist of scornful amusement that woke a traitorous admiration in Kereka's heart. Someday she, the *begh*'s daughter who wished to live a man's life, would look upon her enemies with that same lazy contempt.

A band of warriors topped a far rise, the sound of their wings fading as they pulled up behind their leader to survey the stones beyond. The captain wore the distinctive metal glitter of griffin feathers on his wings, their shine so bright it hurt the eyes. They carried a banner of deep night blue on which rose a sword moon, dawn's herald.

"Belek," Kereka whispered, sure he could not see them, "it's the Pechanek! Curse them!"

Belek coughed and moaned; turned his head; kicked his feet in frustration.

She, too, struggled. Bad as things were, they had just gotten worse. Belek was healed; if they could escape or talk their way free, they had a hope of riding out again to continue Kereka's hunt, or maybe tricking their captors into a moment's inattention that would allow Kereka to kill the bearded man. Tarkan's bones! How had the Pechanek come to this forsaken place? Only a man who had killed a griffin had earned the right to wear griffin's wings. The *begh* of the Pechanek clan was not such a man. But his son Vayek was.

No *begh*'s son of a rival tribe would be out looking for three youths who must, after all, make their own way home or be judged unworthy of manhood's privileges and a man's respect. Had all her attempts to train herself in secret with her brother's aid in weapons and hunting and bragging and running and wrestling and the crafts and knowledge reserved for men now come to nothing?

A bitter anger burned in Kereka's throat. Her eyes stung, and for an instant she thought she might actually burst out of her bonds from sheer fury, but the magic binding her was too powerful.

The leader raised his spear to signal the advance. They raced out, wings singing, and split to encircle the stones. Waiting at a distance, they watched as their leader trotted forward alone. He was that sure of himself. His gaze scanned the stones, the two foreigners, the corpse, and the prisoners. Spotting Kereka, he stiffened, shoulders taut. He bent slightly forward, as if after all he had not expected to find her in such a predicament.

He absorbed the shock quickly enough. He was a man who knew how to adapt when the tide of battle turned against him; his cunning retreat in the face of superior numbers that he had twisted into a flanking ambush as the enemy galloped in reckless pursuit had defeated the Torkay, a tale everyone knew. He swung his gaze away from Kereka and addressed the bearded man, punctiliously polite.

"Honored sir, I address you. I, who am Prince Vayek, son of the Pechanek *begh*, scourge of the Uzay and Torkay clans, defender of Tarkan's honor, Festival champion, slayer of griffins. If you please, surrender. Therefore, if you do so, we will be able to allow you to live as a slave among us, treated fairly as long as you work hard. If we are forced to fight you, then unfortunately we must kill you."

"You are not the man who arranged to meet me here," said the woman, her voice so resonant and clear that it seemed the wind spoke at her command. Had she always known their language? For unlike the foreigners enslaved by the clans, she spoke without accent, without mistake, as smoothly as if she had taken someone else's voice as her own.

Belek coughed again, and Kereka glanced his way as he opened and closed his mouth impotently. Was this the payment—or maybe only the first of many payments—the witch had ripped out of him? Had she stolen his voice?

"Women are consulted in private, not in public among men," Vayek continued, still looking toward the bearded man. "I do not wish to insult any woman by so boldly addressing her where any man could hear her precious words."

"Alas, my companion cannot speak your language, while I can. Where are my griffin feathers? For I perceive you have them with you, there, in that bundle." She gestured with the crossbow.

Kereka had all this time been staring at Vayek, not because the conical helm seemed shaped to magnify and enhance the shapely regularity of his features but rather as a dying person stares at the arrow of death flying to meet her. But now she looked in the direction of the gesture to see one horse whose rider was slung belly-down over the saddle, a bulky bundle of rolled-up hides strapped to his back.

Fool of a stupid girl! How was she to free herself if she could not pay attention, observe, and react? She was still on the hunt. She wasn't married yet.

Vayek's warband rode with a dead man. And it was this man, apparently, who the witch had been waiting for. Kereka and the others had merely had the bad fortune to stumble upon their meeting place.

"I am willing to pay you the same reward I offered to the man I first dealt with. I presume that the bundle on his back is what he was obliged to deliver to me."

Vayek struggled; he truly did. He was famous among the clans for his exceptional courtesy and honor, and he made now no attempt to hide his feelings of embarrassment and shame, because true warriors expressed rage and joy and grief in public so that others might live their own struggles through such manly display. He looked again toward the bearded man, but the bearded man made no effort to intercede.

"Very well." As unseemly as it was to engage in such a conversation, he accepted the battleground, as a warrior must. "I will speak. I pray the gods will pardon me for my rudeness. I discovered a Berandai man skulking westward through the land with this bundle of griffin feathers. It is forbidden to trade the holy feathers outside the clans. He has paid the penalty." He gestured toward the body draped over the horse. "How can it be that such a meeting transpired, between foreign people and a plainsman, even one of the lowly Berandai, who like to call themselves our cousins? How can any foreigner have convinced even one of them to dishonor himself, his clan, and the grass and sky that sustains us?"

"Have your ancestors' tales not reminded you of that time, long in the past, when the Quman clans as well as the Berandai and the Kerayit made an agreement with the western queen?

When they sent a levy to guard her, so the sorcerers of their kind could weave paths between the stones?"

"Women do not rule over men. We clansmen do not send our warriors to serve foreigners as slaves."

But Kereka had seen the flash of light in the stones. Could it be true that the witch and her companion had used sorcery to weave a path into these stones from some other faraway place? That they could cross a vast distance with a single step? The old tales spoke of such sorcery, but she had never believed it because the Quman shamans said it could not be accomplished. Yet what if they had only meant that *they* could not weave such magic?

"Maybe *you* do not remember," the witch went on, "but some among you have not forgotten the old compact. This man had not. He was one among a levy sent into the west by his chiefs ten years ago. I saved his life, but that is another story. His debt I agreed could be repaid by him delivering to me what I needed most."

"But I have already declared that it is forbidden! Perhaps an explanation is necessary. Griffin feathers are proof and purchase against sorcery. They are too powerful to be handled by any man except a shaman or a hero. They cannot be allowed to leave the grasslands. Long ago, griffin feathers were stolen from our ancestors, but the fabled *begh* Bulkezu invaded the western lands and returned the stolen feathers to their rightful place."

"Bulkezu the Humbled?" Her laughter cut sharply. "I see your clans do not learn from the past, as ours do in our careful keeping of records."

"Bulkezu was the greatest of *beghs*, the most honored and respected! He conquered the western lands and trampled their riders beneath his feet, and all the people living in those days knelt before him with their faces in the dirt."

She snorted. "He died a hunted man, killed by the bastard prince, Sanglant of Wendar. How small your world is! What tales you tell yourself! You don't even know the truth!"

Belek squirmed and grimaced, looking at Kereka with that excitable gaze of his, full of the hidden knowledge he had gleaned from the shamans who favored him and had shared with the sister he loved so well that he had secretly taught her how to fight.

She was accustomed to silence in the camp, but the witch's confident tongue emboldened her: *how small your world is.* Her own voice was harsh, like a crow's, but she cawed nevertheless, just to show that not all Quman were ignorant and blind. "I heard a different tale! I heard the great *begh* Bulkezu was killed by a phoenix, with wings of flame!"

Vayek's bright gaze flashed to her, and maybe he was shocked or maybe he simply refused to contradict her publicly before his waiting men because such correcting words would shame them both. Maybe he just knew better than to reveal to his enemy that he knew their prisoners. No doubt he was waiting to attack only for fear of risking Kereka's life. He himself need not fear the witch's sorcery; with his griffin wings, he was protected against it.

"Lads," he said instead, pretending not to recognize Kereka in her male clothing, "where did the witch come from?"

"Prince Belek was already wounded." Kereka choose her words slowly. Through desperate and thereby incautious speech, she and her brother had already betrayed their chiefly lineage, so all that was left them was to conceal Vayek's interest in her specifically. Yet she could not bear for Vayek to think she had given up, that she was returning meekly to the clans having failed in her hunt. "He was wounded taking a head. We had to help him reach his father the *begh* so he could die as a man, not a boy. Any other path would have been dishonorable. When we were riding back, we saw a flash of light like the sun rising. After that, we saw the witch standing up among the stones. We didn't see where she came from."

"Prince Vayek!" the witch cried, laughing as would a man after victory in wrestling bout. "And this lad, the one whose spirit is woven with magic, he too is a prince!" Her gaze skipped from Belek to Kereka, and as the woman stared, Kereka did not flinch; she met her gaze; she would not be the first one to look away! But the woman's lips curved upward, cold and deadly: she was no fool, she could weave together the strands lying before her. She looked back toward the *begh*'s son. "Why are you come, Prince Vayek, son of the *begh* of the Pechanek clan, scourge, defender, champion? How have you stumbled across my poor comrade who so dutifully gathered griffin feathers for me? Were you out here in the western steppe looking for *something else*?"

He could not answer in words: he was too intelligent to give Kereka away, too proud to show weakness in public, too honorable to reply to a charge cast into the air by a woman who by all proper custom and understanding must be deemed insane and her life therefore forfeit.

He was a hero of the clans, seeking his bride. He had a different answer for his enemies.

He signaled with his spear. His riders shifted from stillness to motion between one heartbeat and the next. His own horse broke forward into a charge.

But the witch had guessed what was coming. She flung a handful of dust outward. When the first grains pattered onto the scarred earth sown with Edek's blood, threads of twisting red fire spewed out of the ground. Their furious heat scorched the grass outside the stones, although within them the air remained cool and the breeze gentle. Within two breaths, her sorcery wove a palisade impossible to breach.

Except for a man wearing griffin wings.

He tossed his spear to the ground and, drawing his sword, rode for the gap, where Edek's body, encased in white fire, did not quite seal the sorcerous palisade.

The bearded man released an arrow, the shot flying through the narrow gap.

Vayek rose in his stirrups and twisted, feathers flashing, and the arrow shredded to bits in the metal wings. He settled back into the saddle, lashing the horse, and with a leap they cleared the opening between the fiery palisade and Edek's burning feet. Again, and again, the bearded man released arrows, and again Vayek's quick reflexes shielded him as the arrows shattered in the feathers. He pressed hard, slamming a sword stroke at the bearded man, who hastily flung up his wooden shield to protect himself, taking such a solid blow that his legs twisted away under him and he stumbled back. Yet he was a strong and canny fighter, not easily subdued; he threw himself behind one of the great standing stones for cover as Vayek pulled the weight of his horse around in the confined corral made by the stones and the ring of sorcerous fire. Carrying a cross-bow, the witch ran down to Edek's body and with her stone knife scraped the drying dregs of his blood out from Edek's head toward the far end of the scar. She meant to close the circle.

Kereka tugged at her ropes, hating this helplessness. All her life she had hated the things that bound her, just as poor Belek had hated his warriors' training so much that their father had once joked angrily that it would have been better had they swapped spirits into the other's body. Now, too—of course!—Belek had given up trying to break free; he had even shut his eyes!

"Belek!" Kereka whispered, hard enough to jolt him. "Is there no magic the shamans taught you? Anything that might help us—?"

Hoofbeats echoed eerily off the stones. She heard the snorting of a horse and then the horse loomed beside her, Vayek himself leaning from the saddle with a griffin feather plucked from his own wings held in his gauntlet. His gaze captured hers; he smiled, the expression all the more striking and sweet for its brevity.

"Boldest among women!" he said admiringly. "You have a man's courage and a man's wit! You alone will stand first among my wives, now and always! This I promise!"

What promises he made, he would keep. How could it be otherwise? He was a hero.

And so he would rescue her, and the tale's fame and elaboration would grow in the telling to become one of the great romantic legends told among the clans: his story, and she, like his noble horse, attendant in it.

A bolt like a slap of awakening clattered on the stone's face above Kereka's head and tumbled down over her body: another arrow. He sliced with the feather toward her. Ropes and magic slithered away. As she collapsed forward, released from the stone, he reined his steed hard aside and clattered off at a new angle to continue the fight. Kereka's hands and shoulders hurt, prickling with agony, but she shoved up against the pain. She had to watch. Movement flashed as a spear thrust from behind a huge stone monolith standing off to her right; steel flashed in reply as Vayek parried with his sword.

Over by the fiery palisade, the witch cursed, rising with blood on her knife, the gap between Edek's head and the scar now sealed. She raised the crossbow and released a bolt, but the missile slammed into stone to the right of the two warriors as they kept moving. She cursed again and winched in another bolt, then spun around as a bold rider tried to push through the remaining gap but was driven back by the intensity of the sorcerous flames.

Vayek fought the bearded man through the stones, using the stones and his wings to protect himself while the bearded man, with the agility of a seasoned fighter, used the stones to protect himself, trying to get close enough to hook his axe into Vayek's armor and pull him off the horse.

But in the end, the foreign man was just that: a man. He was not a hero. He was already bleeding from several wounds. It was only a matter of time before Vayek triumphed, yet again, as victor. What glory he would gather then!

All for him, because that was how the gods had fashioned the world: hawks hunted; horses grazed; marmots burrowed;

flies annoyed. A man hunted glory while a woman tended the fires.

So the elders and shamans said. Their word was truth among the clans.

What tales they told themselves! How small was their world?

Legs burning as with a hundred pricking needles, Kereka staggered to the pile of gear and grabbed the haft of the griffin's feather Edek had found. Where her skin brushed the lower edge of a vane, blood welled at once. She grabbed the first leather riding glove that came to hand and shoved her bleeding hand into it, and even then the griffin feather bit through it; tugged on a gauntlet—Edek's—and at last she could grasp it without more blood spilling. She sliced Belek free and hauled him up, the farmer's head bumping against his thigh, still tied to his belt. She shoved him toward the flames consuming Edek's corpse.

"Run! Quickly!" She pushed him before her, and after a few clumsy steps he broke away from her and, clutching his belly, limped in a staggering run as he choked down cries of pain. Kereka easily kept pace beside him, and as the witch swung around, braids flying, bringing her crossbow to bear, Kereka leaped in front into the line of fire.

"Do not kill us!" she cried, "and in exchange for my brother's life and his debt to you, I will fetch you the griffin feathers you seek. I swear it on the bones of my father's father! I swear it on the honor of Tarkan's arrows."

A sword rang, striking stone, and sparks tumbled. A male voice shouted; a thump was followed by the straining howls of men grappling.

The witch stepped aside.

With the griffin feather held before her to cut away the searing heat of the palisade, Kereka dragged Belek through the breach. The cool breeze within the stones vanished and they ran through a haze of hot smoke and blackened grass to burst coughing and heaving into clearer air beyond. The sky throbbed with such a hollow blue like the taut inside of a drum that she wondered all at once what the sky within the stone circle had looked like. Had it even been the same sky? She looked back, but smoke and the weave of fire obscured the area.

The Pechanek men closed around them, spears bristling, faces grim.

"Don't harm us!" Belek cried. "I'm the son of the Kirshat *begh*!"

She gave Belek a shove that sent him sprawling in the grass. Waving the griffin's feather, she shouted in her crow's voice.

"The foreign witch is almost vanquished, but her magic must be smothered once and for all! I come at Prince Vayek's command to take to him the bundle of griffin feathers he captured. At once!"

Women did not command warriors. They sat beside their fathers, or brothers, or husbands, and a man knew he must listen to the advice they dispensed lest he suffer for having foolishly ignored female wisdom. Yet a *begh*'s daughter cannot be trifled with, however unseemly her behavior. Nor would a common warrior wish to offend the future wife of his future *begh*.

The horse with its corpse and cargo was brought swiftly, the thick bundle wrapped in leather cut free. She grabbed the cords and hoisted the bundle onto her back, its weight oddly light given the power of what lay concealed within. Brandishing the griffin feather to cut a path for herself through the witch's sorcery, she ran back into the smoke before they could think to question her, although which one would have the courage to speak directly to her, who was neither kin or wife, she could not imagine. Grass crackled beneath her feet; soot and ash flaked and floated everywhere; the tapestry of flames rose as if to touch the pastures of the heavens, but she did not hesitate. She plunged into the maelstrom of scalding magic. Stinging hot ash rained on her cheeks and forehead.

"Sister! Don't leave me!"

But her and Belek's lives had been severed on the day Prince Vayek had ridden into the Kirshat clan with her bride price. It was the only reason cautious Belek had agreed to let her hunt with him: he was more afraid of losing her than of being beaten for taking her along where no one intended her to go.

Blessed breathable air hit her chest so unexpectedly that she was gulping and hacking as tears flowed freely. She blinked hard until she could see.

At the far edge of the circle, Vayek had caught the bearded man and pinned his axe against stone with his spear. The witch, her back to Kereka, loosed a bolt toward his magnificent profile, but he could not be taken by surprise. He twisted to bring his wings around to shield himself, and with the motion cut his sword down on his hapless prey.

The bearded man crumpled.

The witch shrieked.

Kereka shoved the bundle against the woman's torso and, when the witch flinched back, grabbed the crossbow out of her hands.

"You're not warrior enough to defeat him!" she cried. "Even I am not that! And there's no glory for me in being dead! Here are your griffin feathers. If you want to escape, pretend to fall at my feet."

She tossed the crossbow to one side as she screamed in as loud a voice as she had ever used. "Husband! Husband! The witch weaves an evil sorcery even now. She means to wither my womb! Hurry! We must escape this wicked, evil trap or I will be barren forever, no sons born from your siring to join the Pechanek clan! Hurry!"

He reined his horse hard away from the stone, casting a glance as swift as an arrow toward her. The bearded man lay slumped along the base of the black megalith. It was too late for him. But not for Kereka.

The witch had not moved, caught in a choice between clutching the precious bundle of griffin feathers or lunging past Kereka for the crossbow.

Kereka tripped her neatly, using a wrestling move she'd learned from Belek, speaking fast as she released her. "If it's true there are paths between the stones, then open a way now with your sorcery. But wait for me! Remember that I have fulfilled a debt and I want payment in return. Remember to trust me."

She leaped back as if fleeing something she feared more deeply than death itself. Vayek thundered up behind her, sword raised for the running kill, but Kereka held her ground with the griffin's feather shielding the witch's body.

"I've killed her!" she shouted. "Your courage has emboldened me! Now it won't be said that you laid hands on a mere woman! Quickly, let us go before her sorcery sickens me! I am so frightened, husband!"

She bolted toward the fire like an arrow released from Tarkan's heavenly bow, praying that Vayek would dismiss the woman as not worthy of his warrior's prowess. She ran, and he followed.

The fire's hissing crackle, the horse's weight and speed and heavy hoof-falls as it plunged toward the wall of fire; the high thrumming atonal singing of the wings in the presence of powerful magic; all this perhaps distracted Vayek as she raced ahead and dashed through that flaming gap in front of him. Fire roared. The smoke poured up to greet her, and because she was only one small human on two small feet, she darted to one side even as the clothes on her back grew hot and began to curl and blacken. He galloped past like the fury of the heavens, not even seeing her step aside because he was blinded by the tale he had long since learned to believe was the only tale in all the world.

But it wasn't true. The world was not the same no matter where you went. She'd seen the truth of that today.

She could follow Vayek back onto the sea of grass into a life whose contours were utterly familiar and entirely honorable. Handsome, brave, strong, even-tempered, honorable, famous among the clans for his prowess, with two secondary wives already although he was not ten years a man, he would be the worst kind of husband. A woman could live her life tending the fire of such a man's life. Its heat was seductive, but in the end its glory belonged only to him.

She spun, feet light beneath her, and raced back through the gap.

To find the witch already in action. She had bound the bundle of griffin feathers to her own back. Now she had her arms under the bearded man's shoulders, trying to hoist him up and over a saddled horse. Kereka ran to help her, got her arms around his hips and her own body beneath him. Blood slicked her hands and dripped on her face, but his rattling breaths revealed that he still lived.

The woman spared her one surprised glance. Then, like a *begh*, she gestured toward the other horses before running to a patch of sandy soil churned by the battle and spotted with blood. She unsheathed her obsidian knife and began, as one might at the Festival dance with Tarkan's flaming arrows, to cut a pattern into the expectant air.

A distant howl of rage rang from beyond the sorcerous fire.

Kereka ran to fetch the three remaining foreign beasts who had come with the witch and the bearded man as well as her own mount. The other horses were already saddled and laded, obedient to the lead. She strung them on a line and mounted the lead mare as an arch of golden fire flowered into existence just beyond the obsidian blade. The witch grabbed the reins of the bearded man's horse and walked under the fulgent threads.

Into what she walked, Kereka could not see. But riding the shore of the river of death was the risk you took to find out what lay on the other side.

Wings sang. The shape of a winged man astride a horse loomed beyond the fire. Vayek burst back past the writhing white fire of

Edek's corpse and into the circle. The complex weave that gave the arch form began to fray at the edges, flashing and shivering.

Griffin feathers are proof against sorcery.

She flung Edek's griffin feather away; it glittered, spinning as on a wind blowing out of the unseen land beyond the arch, while Edek's gauntlet fell with a thud to the dirt. Then she whipped her mount forward, and they charged into a mist that stank of burned and rotting corpses, of ash and grass, of blood and noble deeds.

Her eyes streamed stinging tears; heat burned in her lungs.

The foul miasma cleared, and she was trotting free down the slope of a hill with blackened grass flying away beneath the horses' hooves and the sun setting ahead of her, drawing long shadows over the grass. The witch had already reached a familiar-looking stream, and she was kneeling beside the body of her comrade as she cast handfuls of glittering dust over his limp form. Saplings and brush fluttered in a brisk wind out of the west.

Kereka twisted to see behind her the same stones, the very same stone circle, rising black and ominous exactly where they had stood moments before. Vayek and his warband had vanished.

Did the witch possess such powerful sorcery that she could pluck men from the present world and cast them into the spirit world?

No.

The carpet of burned grass had cooled; its ashy stubble had been disheveled by strong winds; green shoots had found the courage to poke their heads above the scorched ground. She dismounted, tossed the reins over her mount's head. Her mare nipped one of the pack horses, who kicked; she separated the steppe horse and hobbled her, then trudged on aching feet back up into the stones.

The soles of her boots were almost burned away. Her clothes shed flakes of soot. Her hands oozed blood from a score of hairline cuts. Her chest stung with each breath she inhaled.

There lay what remained of Edek, flesh eaten away by the unearthly fire and skeleton torn and scattered by beasts. Cut ropes lay in heaps at the base of three stones; the litter had been mauled by animals but was mostly intact. Their gear was gone, picked up to the last knife and bridle and leather bottle. The ashes of the campfire were ground into the earth. The wind gentled as dusk sighed down over them.

The moon shouldered up out of the east, round and bright, the full moon on which she was to have been wed. The moon could not lie. Half a month had passed since the night of the sword moon. The witch had woven a path between that time and this time, and they had ridden down it.

A whistle shrilled. Standing at the edge of the stones, Kereka saw the witch, standing now and waving to catch her attention. Trusting fool! It might well be easy to kill her and take the bearded man's head while he was injured and weak, before the witch fully healed him, if he could be healed. She could then ride back to her mother's tent and her father's tribe and declare herself a man. She knew what to expect from a man's life, just as she knew what a woman's life entailed.

So what kind of life did these foreigners live, with their sorcery and their crossbows and the way they handed a shovel from one to the other, sharing the same work, maybe even sharing the same glory? It was a question for which she had no answer. Not yet.

She went back to the litter and grabbed the leather tow lines. Pulled them taut over her own shoulders and tugged. Like uncertainty, the burden was unwieldy, but she was stubborn and it was not too heavy for her to manage.

Could she trust a witch? Would a witch and a foreigner ever trust her?

Pulling the litter behind her, she walked across the charred earth and down through the tall grass to find out.

From
Russia, with Love

C.E. MURPHY

Their mistake was in desiring my mother's daughter.

No: let me start at the beginning, when I listened to foolish men make foolish jests that turned, as these things always do, to even more foolish action.

I was a barmaid, not for the money, which was poor, but for the ear to the ground; for the hearing of secrets told and of visitors arriving. My mother likes to know these things, but she is fearsome, and her hut with its chicken legs follows her wherever she goes, so she cannot easily spy. I am a simpler creature, only the daughter of a man my mother later ate, and hardly a witch at all.

They came into our smelly little pub as a pair, the two of them dressed so fine and looking so clean. We lived on the edge of Moscow, my mother and I—at least for now, while her house was content to settle there—and the little bar where I found work was not a place that men such as these came to visit.

The taller was red-haired and jade-eyed, and wore a coat of many colors. He smiled or laughed at everything, but his presence took the laughter of the men around him. He was a weight in the air, heating it, and even when he didn't drag on a thin-rolled cigar, hazy blue smoke seemed to follow him.

The other man was smaller, black-haired and black-eyed, altogether ordinary beside his tall companion. I preferred the redhead's easy, dangerous laughter from the start: perhaps it's because I'm my mother's daughter that I like to play with fire. They say flame will defeat her, but I know the thing which has that power, and it is not the heart of man's red flower.

None of that matters now: that is not the story I am trying to tell. I am telling the story of handsome Janx and small dapper Daisani, who wore somber colors to hide from attention. I would say such a man should choose his friends more carefully, because to be friends with a brightly-plumed bird such as Janx is to draw attention, but I *am* my mother's daughter, and I could see that it was more than friendship that kept these two men together. They needed each other the way the light needs the dark, the way fire needs air: not gladly, but deeply, a bond which only the end of time could break.

They were too finely dressed for our wretched dark pub, but they were free with their coin and made new friends quickly: grubby men eager to tell tales that would keep the beer flowing. So it was no surprise to me to hear stories of my mother, for people like to frighten themselves with whispers of witches when they're sober, and even more when they're drunk.

"She eats men alive," one man said, and that was true, so I said nothing.

"She flies on a giant mortar," said another, and that too was true, so again, I said nothing.

"Her house has chicken legs and goes where it wants," said another, and once more spoke truth, and I held my tongue.

"Her daughter is the most beautiful woman in the world," said the first, and now too many things had been said, and so I said, "But Vasili, you tell me *I* am the most beautiful woman in the world," and he spread his arms and spilled his grog and said, "Why then you are Baba Yaga's daughter, and I bet neither of these fine lords can win your heart."

The red-head turned to me with his eyes alight, and bowed with all the grace of a man born to dancing and fine wines and sword lessons. He drew breath to speak, and the other said, "You have business here, Janx, and if you take time to play at women you will lose," which was how I came to know Janx's name.

"I never lose," Janx said with playful boldness, and what his tone told me was that he never imagined he would lose.

His friend said, "Shall I remind you of London?" and Janx turned from the bar and from me with a flash of emerald in his gaze: a flash of fire, for all that its color was green.

"We both of us lost in London, old friend." There was warning in the last two words, making them entirely other than what they seemed. "We both of us lost, and you're the one who chose to follow me to Moscow, so don't lecture me on business or loss."

"I go where there are promises of riches," Daisani said, and though they'd been speaking my language all along, he suddenly sounded as though he ought to be, deep rich avarice in the rolling words.

"And who better to lead you there than me." Janx came back to me and leaned across the bar to offer a sly wink and a promise that might have fallen from a gypsy's lips: "No woman would choose to love when she knew a bet had been placed on the winning, and so I foreswear all wagers in the matter of your heart. I can't speak to the beauty of every woman in the world, but I'll tell the truth and say you're the loveliest woman I've come upon in Russia. If Baba Yaga is your mother indeed, then her greatest magic is in giving the world a beautiful daughter."

I should not have, but I smiled, and I thought I had better not tell my mother what he had said. Mother is jealous of her magics, and if she thought I was the greatest of them, she'd eat me up like she did my father, to have them back inside her.

"Janx," Daisani said again, with more impatience, and Janx said, "*Eliseo*," which was the name I first heard for the smaller man, though in time, as his fame grew, I too came to think of him as Daisani.

"Forgive my friend," Janx said to me. "He's long since misplaced a sense of humor." Then, curiously: "Are you Baba Yaga's daughter?"

A fit came upon me, as sometimes happens; a fit that is the price of being my mother's daughter. Instead of a yes or a no, this is what spilled from my lips: "That depends. Are you a son of the serpent at the heart of the world?"

Both mens' gazes snapped to me, and this, I think, was the moment when things went wrong indeed.

The danger was twofold: one, that I had never seen such passion in men's eyes, and two, that I had never felt such heat rise in me in response. Oh, I had known my share of lovers: Russian nights are long and cold and unlike my mother, I do not eat men when I'm done with them, so I have spent some time in the throes of need. But never like this, nothing so raw it tore through me and left me eager to snatch at these men, to taste them and swallow them whole and make them part of me; and that was when I wondered if my mother had begun this way.

I did not think. I only put out a hand, and the coal shovel by the fire—an old thing, blackened with use—leapt to my fingers and I jumped onto it, not astride, but as one might stomp a spade into the earth—and commanded it whisk me away up the chimney.

Later, I knew this to be a mistake. First, I could never return to work at my wretched little pub, for now they knew me to be Baba Yaga's daughter indeed, but second, and more importantly, I ran. For men such as Daisani and Janx, there is nothing more exciting than the chase.

Beneath the uproar from astonished Russians, Janx turned to Daisani with a smile bordering on beatific, the expression of a man proven so thoroughly right that nothing in this world could upset his smug superiority. "I believe I've found my mark."

"Baba Yaga is a story made to frighten children and pass the long winter nights," Daisani said. "You should know better."

"And you, of all people, should know not to dismiss stories of witches in the forest and demons in the dark. Go away, if you want. I intend to make Moscow mine, and so require the most priceless of baubles to draw my rival away."

"'Your rival.' I know his name is Rumi. After all this time, you still won't speak their names to me first."

"No more than you would tell me the names of your brethren," Janx said easily, then paused. "Would you?"

Daisani snorted, and with no more discussion they left the pub and walked into the frozen winter night. Their breath caught in the air, turned to silver glitter, and faded behind them. "Moscow. Russia is cold, Janx. Why here?"

"You follow me to the ends of the earth and only now ask why?" Janx sauntered along in silence a little while, then shrugged. "Because my kind aren't inclined to go where it's cold, and yet Rumi has been here centuries. He must guard a trinket of tremendous value to make him stay, and I simply can't bear the idea of not having it myself."

"So you'll trade away Baba Yaga's daughter?"

Janx blinked in astonishment. "Her daughter? Don't be silly, Eliseo. Give over that jewel of a girl to anyone else? No, old friend, I intend to make a bargain or a bounty of the old witch herself. None of us has such a prize in our hoards, and who knows what might be done with a witch's bones?"

"The same that might be done with a dragon's," Daisani said dryly. "If you can capture her, why give her up?"

Jade sparkled in the taller man's eyes and Daisani dropped his chin to his chest with a sigh. "You're a fool, Janx."

"But an adventuresome one," Janx said happily. "And since you're here, you can help me. You have her scent?"

Daisani looked insulted, but Janx waved it off. "Go on, track her home. You're faster by far than I am, and much more subtle."

Insult faded, then turned to chagrin. Daisani thinned his mouth. "I should know better than to fall for your flattery."

"You do know better." Janx smiled again, the same beatific expression. "But at the end of the day, you can't stand to not be a part of intrigues, and so you're going to go anyway. Besides, if I take wing Rumi will know I'm here, and I'm not willing to give up that advantage just yet. I need you, old friend." He placed a hand over his heart, green eyes wide with pleading. "Without you I have no hope."

"I'm mad," Daisani said, but then there was nothing at Janx's side but a breeze, and snow blurring into the air along a trail cut too fast for the eye to see.

It was Daisani who caught me, and he should not have been able to do that. No: not caught; he did not capture me, but when the magic fled from my coal shovel and I came to rest at the forest's edge—for I have not got my mother's strength, and metal and iron will only defy the world's pull for so long at my command—when I came to rest, small unhandsome Eliseo was at my side as though we'd walked all the way together. He twirled his fingers like a man presenting a flower to his beloved, and though nothing was there, I thought I saw a rose of silver and ice catch the moonlight and scatter shards through the frozen night air. I plucked the imaginary flower from his fingers and tucked it above my ear, seeing it all white and shining against the blackness of my hair.

A gift: I should not have taken a gift from a man such as this, but doing so made me smile. "Who are you?" I asked then, "and what does it mean to be a son of the serpent at the heart of the world?"

Daisani tilted his head, giving him the look of a curious sparrow, even to the black glitter of his gaze. "Like for like," he said. "How does Baba Yaga's daughter know to ask, but not know what it means?"

Well. I was not going to answer that, and so could not demand my own answer. We stared at one another, he and I, until a smile curved his mouth. "Janx is here to collect a trinket for his treasure chest."

Anger flared in me, though wit told me not to rise to such bait. Still, I was no trinket, and Eliseo saw my outrage in the set of my jaw. "And you are here because you and he are bound by time and love and loathing," I said before he could banter on. "What's a trinket to him is a triumph to you, if you can steal it before he does. I'm neither to either of you."

"Ah," he said, so lightly, "and yet you already wear my flower in your hair."

I reached to crush the imaginary bloom, but was stopped by Eliseo Daisani's cold kiss. For an instant I was breathless, and then I was alone in the dark.

⚛

"You have a stink on you," my mother said as I came into her house. This was the trouble of being her daughter: there were no secrets, even ones I might have liked to keep. "Blood and sex and magic, and none of it made of mortal flesh. Go," she said, without care to the ice drops forming in the air outside. "Wash yourself, or the house will eat you up. Come back when you don't stink, and I will gnaw a bone and tell you of the serpent at the heart of the world."

I stared at her, a bent and ancient crone with sharp teeth and sharper eyes, and thought of the illusory rose and the brief kiss on my lips; of the magic I'd used to run away; and then I went, the obedient daughter, to scrub myself with snow.

There is no good way to wash in a Russian winter: it is all cold and miserable, and best done wearing boots and nothing else. I might have dragged the tub from the house's tiny porch inside and let its packed snow melt in front of the fire, but neither my mother nor the house would bear my stink that long, so I crouched under the house and washed quickly, my face stuck in a grimace against the cold.

"Eliseo's maligned me," Janx murmured, light voice coming from darkness. He should not have followed me, no more than Eliseo, and not with more daring than Eliseo had shown. Eliseo, at least, had only caught me at the city's edge, where Janx slipped into Baba Yaga's territory, and seemed not to worry a whit. I went still, clutching my handful of scrubbing snow, a bit of prey hoping not to attract her predator's attention. But then, I was my mother's daughter, not prey, so made myself bold enough to stand and face him.

He smiled and looked me all over in the moonlight. His gaze weighted me, warmed me, until I thought the frozen air had thawed even though my skin remained puckered and tight with cold. My skin, yes, though heat wakened in other parts of me, and I would have to scrub all over again to rid myself of this new stink. But he was beautiful in the half-light, a scent of cigar smoke rolling through the thin air toward me as he pulled the tub from the porch and let it thump against the ground. "It's true I come seeking trinkets, but you're not one I'd bargain for. I made you that promise at the pub."

"Why are you here?" I had an answer to that, one that made the warmth inside me conquer the frigid air, and every part of me knew that it was not wise to keep speaking with him. That I should call out to my mother, warn the house; that I should let them do as they would with the red-haired man who stood before me. Indeed, a thought trickled into my mind, that Mother and house alike should already know of his presence, that one or the other should have swept down by now to gobble him up. That neither had happened only interested me further, as though I needed something beyond the dark light in his gaze and the slim fine lines of his body to command my attention.

"There are things I need from you, and others I desire." Rue curved his mouth, amusement colored his eyes: we might have been in a ballroom, dancing with words as much as bodies, both knowing we said more than we should and less than we wished. At least, so I imagined: I knew little of ballrooms, and more than I wanted of wishes.

"Tell me what you need," I said unwisely, "and I'll give you what you desire."

Janx smiled his insouciant smile and crouched by the tub packed with snow, putting his fingers in it. Steam hissed from the snow and melting began to spill away from his hand. I came forward, all heavy boots and cold skin, to shovel more snow into the tub with my hands, until I could step out of my boots and into scalding water.

It splashed over the sides of the tub and made ice of the snow around it as Janx joined me, and in a very little while I thought that my mother could tell me nothing, that I had learned all I needed to know of the serpent in the heart of *my* world.

That, then, was when he asked me how to capture a witch.

I laughed, of course, and perhaps it was the sound of laughter that brought my mother from her house. She is old and crafty, and knows that when love turns to laughing, lovers are easily caught unawares. Not I: I was only surprised she had taken so long to come to us. Janx, though; well, Janx knew nothing of my mother, and was bold besides.

He stood up from behind me, stepped out of the tub, and in the moonlight against the snow he was golden, a liquid metal god with hair blackened by water spilling over his shoulders. Snow melted around his feet, though ice would capture him soon enough if he stopped moving. As for myself, I wished my clothes were nearer, and huddled in the water to hide from cold I hadn't felt while in his arms.

Mother held a bauble in one hand, a thread with a blood-colored pendent dangling from it. She lifted it high and the pendant's thin gold wire caught in the moonlight, making sharp lines across her gnarled knuckles. "Witches," she said to Janx, "are no easier to catch than dragons, but like dragons, we look fondly on gifts. I can count back centuries, and in all that time

I can think of no gifts brought to me by the one who calls Moscow his own."

I lifted wet fingers to wet hair, remembering the rose Eliseo hadn't given me, and wondered what my mother would make of that.

"I would give you all his trove save one piece," Janx offered. His head tilted, gaze gone to the crimson pendant, and a quickness came into his voice; an urgency that I hadn't heard as missing when he'd wanted me, but now that I knew its sound, it left me cold and alone with regret. "All but the piece that keeps him here, and that one would be mine."

"Spoils of war are no fit gift," Mother said dismissively. She raked him with a glance and a fit of avarice came into her eyes, a look I knew well enough, for it had been my own not so long ago. I opened my mouth to whisper a warning, but the words stuck in my throat, and that was no doing of my own.

"I know little of witches," Janx said, "and less of how your magics work. But I have three books, taken from three sisters three hundred years ago. Perhaps they'd suit your tastes."

"The grimoires of Birnam Wood," Mother murmured, and bumps stood up on my skin in the cooling water. I knew those books, as anyone who was my mother's daughter might. As any of the old ones might, but there are few of them left now, and their daughters are not what their mothers might have hoped.

"Yes," Mother whispered, "that will do. Come, red lord, let me grant you thanks in exchange." The jeweled wire glittered again, and Janx walked forward, a king to be crowned, and bent his head so she might drop the shining thing around his neck.

"A ruby," she said, "bled white in my fist and filled with color again by a virgin's blood."

Janx lifted the stone from against his naked chest and admired it in the moonlight. "I'm no unicorn to be caught by a maiden, old mother."

"Not," my mother said, and the weight of it shivered cold out of the air, "unless the maiden is a witch."

Tension sluiced into Janx's shoulders, and not until it arrived did I realize how little worry he carried in his body. Men were not like that; they moved with strain that belied natural grace, but nothing of concern had marred his form until now. Then something more happened, something unlike any I had ever seen, and that even without it coming to pass properly enough *to* see.

For a violent instant two beings occupied the space he stood in. One was the slim long-legged man whose beauty had caught my eye; the other was a savage thing, impossible in size, struggling to burst through the shape I'd come to know. It was a thing of fire and fury, of burnished color and changeable smoke, blurring, vibrating, unseeable in its struggle to change. Fear should have wakened in me, but instead my breath caught and I knew I had learned nothing of the serpent, after all.

Then the attempt was over and Janx flinched toward me, panting, agape with disbelief and anger. He clawed his fingers at the necklace, and though strain pulled the muscle in his arm, the chain refused to break. "You were no—"

Shame filled my chest. "Not now, but I was once, and my mother does not waste what tools she has at hand." I stood and called my clothes to me with a whisper of power, much less than it took to ride a coal shovel across the edges of a city, and shivered into layers and furs before looking to Janx again. His jade eyes were wide, no longer drinking me up, but searching for answers in my hidden form.

"It was not a trap," I said heavily. "I thought we might steal a while without my mother knowing. But we are beneath her house, and nothing passes here that she doesn't see." Gaze lowered, I stepped past him, but he caught my arm with a fingertip touch. Compulsion brought my eyes to his, and if he had not been chained by my mother's will I might have thought that compulsion to be one he laid on me. But no: it came from within, burgeoned by apology, seeking forgiveness.

Humor and confidence shone in his face: an obvious lie. I was my mother's daughter, and could see fear tight against his bones, could see anger burning emerald in changeable eyes. But there was nothing of falsehood in the words he breathed: "Some things are worth risking all."

His smile left a mark in my mind, a scar that would never fade, and as I climbed the ladder into my mother's house, I heard her whisper, carried on the thin winter air: "And now you know why White Rumi has never left this place. You, though, will go. Change your form and fetch me my grimoires. I command it."

An infuriated roar and an upheaval beneath it sent the house to scrambling, looking for safe ground to stand upon, and when I looked out the window it was to see a blazing fiery arrow climbing into the sky.

A slash of white flew upward, a meteorite falling in reverse. It slammed into the streak of red that was Janx, and Daisani, sitting at the forest's edge hundreds of feet below, sighed and put his palm to his forehead.

The dragons alone fought territory wars. They alone knew when another of their kind took their Old shape nearby, tasting it as a challenge in the air. The youthful among them—when there had been young—transformed often, struggling to steal or win a scrap of land for their own, and then to hold off other comers. It was the way of the young.

Janx, though, had not been young for a long time.

Knowing what he'd see, Daisani dropped his hand and turned his attention to the stars again. They fell, the two dragons in the sky: they fell writhing and spitting and tangling with each other, toward rooftops that housed men sleeping for the night. That was lucky: mankind's population grew too quickly for red Janx, for white Rumi, for any of them to take the kind of risk these two did now, and its only saving grace was that the hour was small and only drunkards would be out in the frozen morning. Daisani wished the moon away and instead watched it catch the brilliance of Rumi's wings as he finally pulled out of the fight to gain altitude again. Janx twisted after him, larger wings driving him higher more rapidly, and even from the distance, Daisani winced as one of Janx's huge clawed feet smashed Rumi in the head and sent the smaller dragon tumbling.

And, against every natural tendency, flew higher still, and cut his way across the night, darkness swallowing him whole. Daisani stared after him, relieved and bewildered. Something had gone wrong with the witch's daughter; that much was clear, but then, that much had been all but promised in the moment she'd called the coal shovel to herself and flew out of the pub. He was no stronger in the face of astonishing events or beautiful women than Janx was: curiosity was a cat to kill them both, though he, at least, he had more sense than to romance the girl at her mother's house.

Fascination bit all the harder with Janx's departure: he couldn't catch a sky-bound dragon, but the other might have answers, and he was still falling toward the earth.

Daisani reached the crash site before Rumi himself did.

Snow smashed upward and caught in the air, fragile glittering bits of light under the moon. Daisani brushed his shoulders clear and climbed a hill of displaced snow, crouching on its crest to examine the fallen dragon.

Blood leaked over the behemoth's eye, a wintery scale torn loose from Janx's kick, and the white whiskers around his mouth looked like silver drool against the snow. He was smaller than Janx, who was of an impossible size, but the same in general form: serpentine, winged, legged, long and slender in all ways. Not even Daisani had often studied a dragon in repose, and he thought the form admirable, if impractical for a world growing more and more populated by man. "Wake up and change back. You idiots may have woken someone, and whatever treasure keeps you here, it won't be worth a dragon hunt."

One of Rumi's eyes peeled open—complex double lids, like a snake—to reveal ice blue before it shuttered closed again. He pushed up on a foreleg with aching care, then rumbled a wordless curse and transformed. Wind rushed by Daisani, knocking his clothes askew, and the echo of transformation left his ears ringing. A white-haired man as tall and slim as Janx sat in the middle of a dragon-shaped depression, and as he stood a ruby pendant on a silver wire slid from beneath his shirt. He tucked it away again, and Daisani watched the impression it made. "I thought the purpose of a hoard was to hide it away unseen."

Rumi scowled, uncertain, then scowled more deeply still. "Vampire."

"And a curious one at that. I've known Janx for more centuries than you've been alive, and in all that time I've never seen him wear decorations. Dragons," Daisani said with easy confidence, "don't. So tell me the story of your silver chain, and I'll be on my way."

Anger worked the dragon's thin mouth, pulling his lips back to show too-long, inhumanly sharp teeth. "I can't," he finally said, and then, more bitterly, "Ask the witch's daughter."

Daisani's eyebrows lifted. "And why would she answer me?"

"She might not." Against all good sense, Rumi slammed back into his dragon form, sound and shockwave powerful enough to send Daisani staggering. "But I *can*not, and so if you want answers, vampire, seek them with her." He flung himself into the air, leaving Daisani still curious and now blanketed in snow.

A week of waiting: not so much time, for one such as Eliseo Daisani. He was a patient predator, though many—most—of his kind were not. The witch and her daughter would go nowhere until Janx returned: that was Daisani's bet, even without a taste of blood to tell him which way the wind blew.

He didn't expect the dragon to return with a leather satchel grasped in gold-dipped talons, nor for Janx's wisdom to have left him altogether. The terrible crimson beast that he was came winging out of hard winter sunshine, scattering so rough a landing that Baba Yaga's house leapt aside to keep from being toppled. That was not Janx; in uncountable centuries Daisani had no memory of the dragonlord risking exposure so blatantly. Under cover of night; under cover of smoke and fog and war: those were the times when a dragon might return to his elemental form and trust that mankind's eyes wouldn't see. They were too large, too dangerous, too obvious a threat; Daisani and his kind could take far greater risks, and as for the others, well: the selkies were drowned, the djinn bound to their deserts, and the gargoyles were night-time creatures and cautious besides. That was the price of being birthed of solid steady stone, though by that logic, fiery dragons might well be the most reckless of all the surviving races.

Janx transformed to human shape entirely naked in the snow, dressed in nothing but an expression of rage and a glint of gold at his throat. The daughter came out from the chicken-legged house to take the satchel from Janx's hands, and the human-formed immortal softened, some of his fury bleeding away at the girl's presence. Daisani, hunched in a tree like an over-sized raven, didn't try to hide his grin: this would be fodder for centuries to come.

"Drowned by water," an old woman's voice whispered in his ear, and all around him, snow splashed to meltwater below the sound of chains rattling. Branches, freed of their heavy white burden, sprang upward and snaked toward him, and rushing water bared black dirt between the tree's toes. "Staked by wood, bound by iron, buried in earth."

Janx's wisdom had fled: Daisani's had not. He dove from the tree and sped across the forest, racing a specter whose words followed him: "Forget the serpent's son, Eliseo Daisani, and I shall pursue you no more."

There was no joy in bedding a man bent to my mother's command. Under her whim he was a lap-dog, not a firebrand, his color leached and his eyes dull except when anger moved him. Then he was stirred to beauty, but the red gem at his breast would flare and he would subside again, leaving me aware that I was a fool and red-haired Janx was lost to me. Emboldened by curiosity and loss, I peeked at the pages of my mother's oldest grimoires, the books of magic which lay down the laws of the world. She might have told me herself, had I asked; might have told me of the serpent at the heart of the world, but I disliked the thought of offering her more power over me. My interest was a thing of my own, and I had little enough of that to want to hoard it. That, and I knew now that dragons were real, and so clinging to precious bits of knowledge had a sweeter taste, as though I could make myself closer to the one I'd inadvertently betrayed by collecting and keeping what wisdom I could.

I let myself pretend I was fooling my mother. It's possible I was, but the heart of me, where I was fully her daughter, said I lied to myself as I'd done when I'd stolen an hour with a dragonlord. That time had not been stolen, no more than my dredges of scholarship were: they were granted me by a witch whose fore-sight ran far beyond mine, and who would find a way to use what little I could eke out and take for my own.

I knew this, and still I didn't care, because what I learned was beautiful.

I had known, of course, that those such as my mother sprang from those places in the earth where confidences were whispered and offerings burnt. They rose up from ashes and secrets, rose up stench-ridden with death and burdened under the promise of silence for sly things shared. They rose up mad things, shaped by their making, greedy for knowledge won at any cost. Frightened peasants told tales that water would not drown a witch but that fire would burn her, and that gave them comfort, false as it was. Only one thing could condemn a witch, and that was exposure of the secret that gave her life. Her first secret: that, and that alone, would undo my mother or any witch. The few old ones who remained had long-since outlived those who'd whispered the first secrets, so long-since that I had thought no one in this world might have been there to watch them birthed.

But now I knew of the Old Races.

If I had been my mother I could have sunk my fingers into the grimoires and drawn the knowledge in through my blood. But we daughters are not what our mothers hoped, and I could only turn page after page, reading hungrily. They were fables, these stories, legends written by the hopeful and the lonely, but they were written in books of magic, and they were written in words of blood.

Dragons. Oh, dragons I knew, in the slim sweet form of the red-haired man my mother held under lock and golden chain.

They were born of the hot places in the world, far from my frozen Russia. Like the witch my mother was, they were greedy for precious things, and this is how dear the knowledge of how to hold a dragon was to my mother's heart: it remained unwritten, even in the pages of her own grimoires. In all the world, she may have been the only witch to bind a dragon, and that, *that* was deep magic indeed.

Vampires. Their gift was speed, and answered for me how Eliseo Daisani had come to stand at my side even after my coal-shovel escape. They, too, could be bound; all of the Old Races could be, though none of them easily, and vampires with the most difficulty of all. Unlike the dragon charm, a vampire's confinement was written in the book, proof enough that amongst the ancient crones it was a spell well-known. What lay unmarked in the history of vampires was their genesis: not even my mother knew where they came from, though someone in the writing of this book had hinted that they were not of this world at all.

There were others, though, so many others. Gargoyles, which my people might have called golems, and seal-folk called selkie which were only stories from the ice-bound hunters who lived even further north than my mother's hut chose to go. Mountain-men called yeti, and water-born sea folk whom popular tales called *mer*, but who were written in these pages as *siryn* who swam with sea serpents. Djinn, which were the living wind, and winged angry women named *harpies*. These were creatures of the darkness, all the dreams and fears of humanity given form, and they were dying.

Some had died to fill these pages. Words wrapped around drawings, and more than one of those scrawled pieces of art writhed when my gaze slipped away. Magic pinned them in place, secrets draining their vitality and preserving them forever, though they would remain known only to a few.

There were wonders in the world; that, I had always known. How could I not, when I was my mother's daughter? But they were greater than I had imagined, and I felt the first stirrings of lust in me as I read my mother's grimoires. Not lust for men, or even dragons, but the burning need to learn more. I wanted to tear the living drawings from the book itself and eat them up, to chew them and taste what they were, to learn it and have it in me for all time. That, then, was the witch in me, and wisdom told me to keep my curiosity's flame low. Baba Yaga is jealous of her knowledge, and if my child's interest turned to active desire in her eyes, she would eat me up and make all my thoughts and questions her own.

A week passed while I read, then two. The light began to return, though winter grew more bitter yet. I thought of Janx at times, but more often I thought of the imaginary rose, and wondered that I had been so wrong, that the man called Daisani could so easily leave his partner behind.

When I left the hut it was to discover I could find no jobs that would have me, now that it was known whose daughter I was. I walked muddy frozen streets, listening for what was to be heard, and this is what I heard: Moscow rumbled with discontent, with too many stories of witches and magic. The poor and superstitious spat when they saw a black-haired woman of beauty, while the rich and fanciful cut those same women deep curtseys and bows, just in case they were Baba Yaga's daughter.

Mother had her grimoires and no other cares: she even put the dragon to sleep, that his grumblings should not bother her. Her other pet, the sullen icy Rumi, came calmer at that, and with his calm the city calmed, as though it had become so much a part of him the one could affect the other. Then only I was left with discontent, hungry for a touch that my mother had neutered and searching for the one who might make it whole again.

When he came it was from the wealthy quarter, and there was a determination beneath the artful lightness of his voice. He played at being Janx, I thought, but Eliseo Daisani was that coin's other side, and the act sat badly with him. Still, he spoke with a touch of romance the dragon hadn't pretended to, and my ears were good enough to hear that there was no pretense as he murmured: "You still wear my rose in your hair."

My fingers flew to the nothingness tucked above my ear, the gesture enough to say his words were truth. We were in a square, broad and empty for all that daylight shone down, and he offered me his elbow like a gentleman. "I have been around the joined continents these past two weeks. Would you like to know what I've learned of witches in that time?"

"I would." My mother would not like whatever answer he gave, but at least I would have it to give her.

Eliseo Daisani nodded and we walked in a long time silence, leaving the rich parts of the city and finding its ragged, forest-ridden edge. "Nothing," he said then, as if the trees had shaken loose his tongue. "I have learned nothing at all. Those few witches old enough to carry knowledge carry too much and are a danger, and the young can only tell me that a man bent to a witch's will is caught beneath a binding spell. I ought to have heeded Rumi, and asked Baba Yaga's daughter first. How do I free my friend?"

"Why would I tell you?"

Daisani smiled. "Because I'll kill you if you don't."

"That's little incentive," I said, and heard myself from a distance; heard myself make a choice that had to do with the fire gone from Janx's jade eyes and the secrets revealed in my mother's grimoires; a choice that spoke to the aching loss in my breast at those secrets caged by a witch's spell. "That's little enough incentive," I said again, and then oh so softly, finished, "for you'll kill me if I do."

My walking partner stopped, a terrible stillness that swept out from him and made him all the things his slight dapper form gave lie to: made him alien and dangerous, made him a killer and a drinker of blood. Then he turned to me, black eyes gone bright, and whispered, "Ah," so that I knew he understood me.

He took my wrist and turned it up, exposing skin to the winter air before tracing a fingertip over blue veins. "Bloodlines," he breathed. "Blood is ever-important."

"It is," I whispered back, "and you will want to run far and fast, Eliseo Daisani. Cross a river and an ocean if you can. Then my mother cannot follow you, for she's a witch bred and born, and running water has its power." By then we were far from the city, lost in a frozen forest, so there was no one who might hear me scream if I chose to. I did not: first, because I thought the heat reborn in Janx's gaze was worth the chill of mine, and second, because—to my surprise—there was no pain. There might even have been seduction, had we willed it, but no: this was a thing done of a duty running deep as mountains reached high, and lust, should it ever come, would come at another time.

It never would come, for me, and as the blood emptied from my body, I felt my heart drawing back what it had once given, calling all parts of me to it so it might keep beating, and in so doing, drained the rubies of their color.

❦

A dragon burst from the chicken-legged hut, scattering its pieces across a snowy landscape. Rage shrieked from the dragon's throat, fire bursting over bits of shattered wood, and below that an ancient crone shrieked too. Agitated chicken legs ran about, their animation comical and terrifying all at once, but no more than the old woman or the pieces of broken house did they burn. Janx hung in the air, spitting fire again and again, until the forest itself was alight, but Baba Yaga refused to burn. Only when her screams cut through his own bellows of insult and fury did Janx take wing to the sky, chased by a witch on her mortar as she shouted, "My daughter! My daughter! My daughter is dead! You will pay, you will burn, you will die!"

A flash of black on the snow below: Janx dove and captured Daisani in gold-tipped talons, and together they fled Russia and the rage of a witch, followed by promises of their doom should they ever return.

❦

I am, you see, my mother's daughter, and it is not only blood that flows in my veins and gives me life. There is magic, too, and it is lucky for me that Daisani slipped me into a cold deep snowbank to bury me when I died, for my mother would have eaten up my body to take the magic back into herself. Then I would be dead indeed, and there would be no one to tell this story the way I could.

But not even Baba Yaga can sniff out a corpse in an ice field in a frozen Russian winter, and her re-made hut had moved on before spring came to Moscow. The earth thawed and a dream came to me: a dream of the serpent at the heart of the world, and the world's heart was a tree, growing up toward me, around me, waking life in an icy body. A tiny woman came from the tree to bend and kiss my brow, and a bond snapped inside me.

Power took its place, the kind that could call a mortar for me to ride as long as I might want; the kind that could bind a man or eat him up; the kind that could steal magic back from others infused with it; the kind that made me my mother's daughter in more ways than blood. I thought of her, and of her house, and of all the stories of fear and warning that rode with her, and I thought of Eliseo Daisani and the one called Janx. They are in the world, shackled like thirst and drink: the one no good without the other, but those are chains they've chosen, and not ones forced upon them.

For myself, I rose up out of the snow no longer my mother's daughter, and that, I think, is enough.

Words
Like Coins

ROBIN HOBB

"First came drought. Then rats. Now it's pecksies." Jami spoke into the darkness of the bedroom.

"And that's why you're afraid to get out of the bed to get a drink of water?" Mirrifen asked. Her sister-in-law's restless tossing in the bed they now shared had wakened the older woman.

"No," Jami said, with a strangled laugh. "It's why I'm afraid to get out of bed and go to the backhouse." She shivered. "I can hear rats squeaking in the kitchen. Where rats go, pecksies follow."

"I've never even seen a pecksie."

"Well, I have! Lots of them, when I was little. And I saw one today. It was under the front steps, staring at me with its horrid yellow eyes. But when I crouched down to see it, it was gone!"

Mirrifen sighed. "I'll light a lamp, and go with you."

Swinging her feet out of the bed and onto the floor in the dark still put a shiver up her spine. Mirrifen wasn't sure she believed in pecksies but she did, emphatically, believe in rats. She tiptoed out to the banked fire in the kitchen hearth and lit the lamp from its embers. The moving flame painted shifting rat-shadows in every corner. The night before last, Jami had stepped on a rat when she got out of bed for water. Jami's feet were already swollen from her pregnancy. A rat bite could have crippled her. Mirrifen hurried back to the bedroom. "Come on. I'll walk you to the backhouse."

"Mirrifen, you are too good to me," Jami apologized.

Privately, Mirrifen agreed, but she only grumbled, "Why Drake and Edric had to take the dog with them, I don't know."

"To protect them when they camp! All sorts of men are on the roads looking for work. I wish they'd all stayed home. I'd feel safer." Jami sighed as she touched her stretched belly. "I wish I could have one solid night's sleep. Did your hedge-witch ever teach you how to make a sleep charm? If you could make one for me—"

"No, dear heart, I couldn't." They moved slowly through the darkened house. "My training only included simple things. Sleep charms are complicated. They have to be precisely keyed to the user. Even so, they're dangerous. Witch Chorly once knew a foolish hedge-witch who tried to make a sleep charm for herself; she finished it, fell asleep and starved to death before she ever awoke."

Jami shuddered. "A pleasant tale to sleep on!"

The kitchen door slapped shut behind them. Overhead, the light of the waxing moon watered the parched fields. Mirrifen inspected the outhouse to make sure no rats lurked inside, and then gave Jami the lantern. Mirrifen waited outside. The clear, starry sky offered no hope of rain. By this time of year, the crops usually stood tall in the fields. Without them, the wide plains of Tilth stretched endlessly to a distant, dark horizon.

No one could recall a worse drought. Thrice the men had planted; thrice the seeds had sprouted and withered. With no hope of a crop, the two brothers had left them, going off in hopes of finding paying work. They needed to be able to buy more seed grain in the hopes that next spring would be kinder. Mirrifen reflected sourly that their husbands would probably have to go all the way to Buck to find work.

Jami emerged from the backhouse. As they shuffled back toward the farmhouse, Jami spoke her darkest fear. "What if they never come back?"

"They'll come back." Mirrifen spoke with false confidence. "Where else would they go? They both grew up on this farm: it's all they know."

"Maybe away from it, they might find easier ways to live than farming. And prettier girls. Ones that haven't been pregnant forever."

"You're being silly. Drake is very excited about the baby. And your 'forever' is nearly over. The full moon will bring your baby." Mirrifen stepped barefoot on a pebble and winced.

"Is that something the hedge-witch taught you?"

Mirrifen snorted. "No. What Chorly taught me was how much water to mix with her rum. And I learned six different places to hide from her when she was drunk. My apprenticeship was the most worthless thing my father ever bought." Chorly should have taught Mirrifen a hedge-witch's skills, how to make potions and balms, how to sing spells and how to construct charms to protect crops from deer or make hens lay more eggs. Instead, the hedge-witch had treated her like a servant and taught her only the most trivial charms and tinctures. Mirrifen's apprenticeship had been spent cleaning the old witch's ramshackle hut and soothing her disgruntled customers. The old woman had drunk herself to death before she had completed Mirrifen's training. Chorly's creditors had turned Mirrifen out of the tumble-down cottage. She couldn't flee back to her father's house, for her brothers had filled it with wives and children. She had thought herself too old to wed, until her brother's wife had told her of a farmer seeking a wife for his younger brother. "Don't have to be pretty, just willing to work hard, and put up with a man who's nice enough but not too bright."

Edric was exactly as described. Nice enough, and kind, with the open face and wondering mind of a boy. Being his wife and helping on the farm had been the best year of her life, until the drought descended.

"A pecksie!" Jami shrieked, jostling her.

"Where?" Mirrifen demanded, but when Jami pointed, she saw only the swaying silhouette of a tuft of grass. "It's just a shadow, dear. Let's go back to bed."

"Rats bring pecksies, you know. They hunt rats. My mother always said, 'Keep a clean house, for if you draw rats, pecksies will follow.'"

Something rustled behind them. Mirrifen refused to look back. "Come. We'd best sleep now if we are to rise early tomorrow."

But when the morning came, Mirrifen rose alone, slipping quietly from Jami's bed. Since the men had left, she had demanded Mirrifen sleep next to her. Jami was barely nineteen, and sometimes it seemed that her pregnancy had made her more childish than womanly. The blankets mounded over her belly. It couldn't be much longer. Mirrifen longed for the birth as much as she dreaded it. She'd never attended a birth, and the closest midwife was a half-day's walk away. "Eda, let all go well," she prayed and drew the door closed.

The rat invaders had left their mark on the kitchen. Pelleted droppings and smears of filth marked the rat trails along the base of the walls. Mirrifen seized the broom and swept the droppings out the door. She stingily damped a rag with clean water and erased the rat tracks. Jami was almost irrational about rats now.

Not that Mirrifen blamed her. The creatures besieged them. No door could be shut tightly enough to keep them out. The ravenous rats gnawed through pantry doors and chewed open flour sacks. They ate the potted preserves, wax seals and all. In the attic, they scampered along the rafters to get at the hanging hams and bacon sides, spoiling what they didn't eat. They attacked the sleeping chickens on their roosts and stole the eggs.

Every morning, Mirrifen discovered fresh outrages. And every morning, she struggled to conceal from Jami how precarious their situation was becoming. When the men had left, Drake had quietly told her the stored food should sustain them through the summer. "And by fall, Edric and I will be back, with a pocket full of coins and sacks of seed grain."

Brave words. She shook her head and let her work routine absorb her. She woke the fire and fed it. She set a pot of water to boil, filled the tea kettle and put it on the fire. She now stored the porridge grain in a big clay pot on the kitchen table, with the chairs pulled away from it. She'd weighted the pot cover with a rock. The rats hadn't gotten into it, but they'd left their ugly traces on the table. Grimacing, she scrubbed them away with the last of the water in the bucket. She left the porridge simmering while she went to her chores.

She counted the chickens as they emerged from the coop. They'd all survived the night, but there were only crushed shells and smeared yolk on the straw inside the nesting boxes. She stood, fists clenched. How had the rats got in? She'd find their hole later today.

She milked both cows, and gave each a measure of grain and a drink from the covered bucket outside the stall before she turned them out to find whatever grazing they could in the dusty pasture. Every day they gave less milk, poor creatures.

The well in the yard had a good tight cover. She unpegged the wooden hatch in the top and swung it open. Dark and the cool of water greeted her. She scowled to see that the edge of the hatch had been gnawed. The rats could smell the water. If they chewed through and drowned in the well, all the water would be spoiled. What could she do to stop them? Nothing. Not unless she sat on top of the well all night and guarded it. With a sinking heart, she knew that was exactly what she would have to do. The creek had gone dry weeks ago. The well was their last source of water. It had to be protected.

The bucket dropped endlessly before she heard the small splash. She jogged the rope up and down until the bucket tipped and took in water. Drake had promised to put up a proper windlass for the bucket, but for now, it was hand-over-hand to haul it up. Every day, its trip was longer as the water receded. Her straining fingers nearly lost their grip when a small gray face suddenly peered at her from the other side of the well cap. Its staring eyes were the color of verdigris. The hands it lifted seemed disproportionately long. The creature cupped them, begging and bared pointed teeth as she mouthed the foreign word. "Please. Please."

Mirrifen set the dripping bucket down. As she stepped back in astonishment, the small creature collapsed.

Cautiously Mirrifen took two steps around the well cap. The pecksie lay where she had fallen. Yes, unmistakably a 'she' now, for her pregnant belly protruded from her bony frame. Mirrifen stared. A real pecksie. Witch Chorly had never bothered to teach her the spells against them. "Not enough of them to worry about now," the sour old woman had declared. "Keep your mind to practical matters. Go chop some kindling. Pecksies! Pesties, I say. Just be glad they're gone."

Her knowledge of pecksies was small. They dressed in leaves, fur and feathers, and would thieve anything they could carry. They detested cats, and some pecksies had webbed feet. They were reputed to be dangerous, but she couldn't recall why. The little creature collapsed by the well didn't look dangerous. Her bark cloth garments contrasted oddly with silvery gray skin. She was half the size of a cat, and thin. She was curled around her pregnant belly and knobs of spine jutted out from her back. Her bare feet were long and narrow. A fine gold chain showed at the nape of her neck.

As if she felt Mirrifen's scrutiny, the pecksie slowly turned her face up. Her chapped lips parted and a small tongue licked uselessly at them. Eyes green as a cat's opened to slits. The pecksie stared up at her, pleading silently. Then her eyes closed again.

Mirrifen didn't pause to think. She dipped a finger in the milk bucket and held it to the pecksie's lips. A drop fell, wetting them, and the pecksie gaped after it, shuddering. Mirrifen dripped milk into the small mouth. Funny little mouth, with a split upper lip like a kitten's. At the third drop, the pecksie blindly seized Mirrifen's fingertip in her mouth and suckled at it. At a hint of pointed teeth, Mirrifen jerked her hand away. The pecksie's eyes fluttered opened. Mirrifen spoke to her. "I'll tip the bucket and you can dip up some with your hands."

The pecksie pulled herself to a sitting position, her belly in her lap. She leaned into the tipped bucket, scooping up handful after handful of milk and slurping it down. When Mirrifen took the bucket away, the creature's diminutive chin was dripping. She ran a red tongue around her mouth. "Thank-you," she rasped. She closed her eyes tightly. Her words were oddly accented. "I thank you. I am bound now. Still, I thank."

"That's all I can do for you, I'm afraid," Mirrifen replied. "Can you walk?"

The little woman shook her head wordlessly. She stretched out one swollen leg. A crusted slash ran the length of it. The flesh around it was puffy. "Rat," she grimaced.

"Sorry," Mirrifen said.

The little woman stared at her. Slowly, she curled up and closed her eyes.

Mirrifen rose. She secured the hatch to the well, took up the water and milk buckets and carried them into the kitchen. The lid on the porridge was dancing wildly. She hooked it off the fire, stirred in milk, and covered it again. She went to the door of Jami's room and eased it open. Jami still slept, curled protectively around her belly. Just as the pecksie had been.

Mirrifen hurried through the house and back to the well. The pecksie still lay there. On the roof, a crow cawed, protesting his prior claim on the carcass. Mirrifen took off her apron, knelt and picked up the pecksie in a fold of the fabric. Silently, she carried her back to the house and into her own bedroom.

She emptied a small chest of the coffers and bags that held the beads, special twines, feathers and carved rods of a hedge-witch. Silly of her to cling to those fragments of a future now passed. She lined the chest with her shawl and set it on the floor. The pecksie revived enough to lift her head and look about doubtfully as Mirrifen set her in it. Then she lay back with her injured leg stretched out straight and closed her eyes. The open collar of her tunic revealed a small charm around her neck. Mirrifen peered at it. She couldn't read it all, but made out the symbol for birth. So. Pecksies used charms, too. She toyed with an idea, then dared herself.

Moving slowly, Mirrifen hovered her hand over the pecksie's leg. After a moment, her palm detected the heat of an infection. It had reached the pecksie's knee. As Mirrifen moved her hand, she sensed fever building in the little woman.

The paraphernalia scattered on the bed beckoned her. Mirrifen surrendered to the impulse. She had never made a fever charm for so small a person. Did she even remember which beads and what order the spindles and rods went in? She carved the beads smaller and separated yarn to get cord of the right weight. A charm had to be precisely tuned to the person it would serve. When she was finished, a fever charm slightly bigger than her thumbnail dangled over the pecksie's makeshift bed. Mirrifen sat watching her sleep. After a few moments, the lines in her brow loosened and she lapsed into deeper rest.

"Mirrifen! Are you here? Mirrifen!"

Jami sounded alarmed. Mirrifen leaped up and hurried to the kitchen. Absorbed in her charm making, she'd forgotten not only Jami but the simmering porridge. "I'm here, Jami!"

"Oh, Mirrifen! I worried when I couldn't find you. You weren't at the cow shed or the chicken house and—"

"There's no need to be frightened. I'm right here."

"That's not it. Look. Just look at the milk bucket."

"What?"

"Don't you see those silvery smears on the edge? That's pecksie dust! A pecksie has touched our milk bucket!"

When she touched it, her fingertip came away smudged silver-gray, like the pecksie's skin. "Wash it off! Wash it off!" Jami wailed.

"Why?" she asked as wiped her hands on her apron. "Is it poisonous?"

"Who can know? They're such dirty, wicked little things!" Jami's arms clasped her belly to shield her unborn child. "I saw one by the chicken shed. It sneered at me, and vanished."

Mirrifen took a breath. "Jami, sit down. I'll get your break-fast." As Jamie sank into her chair, Mirrifen asked, "How do you know so much about pecksies? I thought they were rare and kept to wild places." She set a bowlful of steaming porridge in front of Jami.

Jami took up her spoon and stirred the boiled grain thought-fully. "When I was little, there were lots of pecksies near our house. My father's land was between a spur of the forest and a sunny little stream, so they had to cross our field to get to water. My mother knew how to use them, so we had them in the house, too. She never realized the danger."

Mirrifen poured water from the kettle over the tea herbs in the pot. "How do you 'use' a pecksie?"

"Oh, it's easy enough. She had to be tricky to snare them, because they know how it works. If a pecksie accepts a favor from you, the pecksie has to do what you ask it. They're bound. Once you have one pecksie, the rest of its clan come around. And a clever woman can trick them into bondage as well."

"I see," Mirrifen said softly. The pecksie's rueful words carried a deeper meaning now.

Jami was caught up in her telling. "There's a lot they can't do, because they're small. They can't sweep, and one almost drowned in our washing tub. But they can fetch eggs and dust, tend the fire, do the sewing, bring vegetables from the garden, weed, and keep rats away. And if you treat them well, they're good natured about it—or so we thought." Jami scowled, remembering. "Perhaps all that time they were hiding their resentment. Is there tea yet?"

Mirrifen poured for both of them. "What happened?"

"They killed my little brothers." Jami's calm voice thickened.

"How?" Mirrifen asked in horror when her silence stretched.

Jami took a breath. "Oh, smothered them, I suppose." Tears clouded her voice. "They were only babies. My mother told the pecksies to watch the baby at night, not to rouse him and to rock him if he woke. So my mother could get some sleep."

Mirrifen nodded.

"Well, one morning, Grag was dead in his cradle. Just dead. Well, everyone knows such things do happen. We mourned him and buried him. Two years later, Mother had another boy. Dwin. He was a fine fat boy. One night she told the pecksies to watch him sleep and call her if he woke. Before dawn, she woke up to all the pecksies standing in a ring around his cradle, squeaking and crying in that horrid way they have. My mother snatched Dwin up, but it was too late. He was dead."

Mirrifen felt cold. She dared not let Jami know that she'd brought an injured pecksie into the house. She had to get rid of it fast. "What did your mother do?"

"She didn't hesitate. All those pecksies had eaten our food and taken favors, so she could command them all. 'Go away!' she shouted at them. 'All of you! Go away forever!' And they went. I watched them stream out of the house, wailing and squeaking as they walked down the road and off into the distance."

"That's all she did?" Mirrifen held her teacup firmly in her trembling hands.

"That's all she needed do," Jami said vindictively. "It meant death for all of them. She knew that. Words bind pecksies. I once heard an old pecksie say that you should spend words like coins.

You can't just say, 'wash the dishes' or they'll wash the dishes all day long. You have to say, 'wash the dirty dishes until they're clean, wipe the dishes until they're dry, and then put them in the cupboard.' They do exactly what you say. So when my mother told them 'Go away!' they had to go and keep going. Forever. Because no one ever gets to 'away', do they? They had to keep walking until they dropped dead in their tracks. My mother knew that. She had learned it from her mother."

A chill squeezed Mirrifen's heart. "And after that?"

"After that, my parents never let a pecksie into the house again. We got cats to keep the rats down. And my parents had three more children, all girls, to my father's sorrow, but they survived because there were no pecksies near their beds. Nasty, vindictive wretches." Jami took a long drink from her cooling tea. When she set her cup down, she looked directly at Mirrifen. "My father always blamed the pecksies for my mother's death."

"What?"

"He found her in the barn, at the bottom of the hay loft ladder. Her neck was broken. She was covered all over in pecksie dust." Jami's voice deepened. "They probably swarmed her and knocked her off the ladder."

"I see," Mirrifen said faintly.

After breakfast, she set a chair outside in the shade, brought Jami her yarn and needles and slipped quickly away to her own room. The pecksie was gone. She'd taken the little charm against infection. Well. Perhaps it was all solved and for the best. She wondered if pecksies were as treacherous as Jami believed, and hoped she would never find out.

The day passed slowly, as every day had since the men had left. Time was measured in what she could not do; no weeds to pull, no vegetables to harvest, no fruit to thin on the parched trees. Idleness today in exchange for want later; a bad bargain all around. She couldn't find any hole in the chicken coop, but when she cleaned it out, three rats boiled up from under the soiled straw. She swept them out with her broom and shut the door tight.

Twice she thought she'd glimpsed the pecksie, but each time, when she turned, nothing was there. She blamed it on Jami's horrid tale and her own imagination and tried to stay busy.

After the evening meal, she washed the dishes and watered the withered kitchen garden with the used wash water. She drew one bucket of water and gave the poor cows their second drink of the day before shutting them in their stall. She shooed the chickens into the cleaned coop and shut their door tightly. Finally, she broke her news to Jami.

"I have to sit up tonight by the well and keep the rats away."

Jami argued, she wept, and then she argued again. "I can't sleep alone in that empty house, with rats rustling in the corners. And pecksies. You saw the pecksie dust on the bucket."

"Well, you can't stay awake outside with me, either. Jami, be sensible. Neither of us have any choice in this."

Jami surrendered, but not with grace. Mirrifen ascribed her sulk to her pregnancy and tried not to mind it. It was hard. After all, she was the one who had to spend the night outside with a club and a lantern. She took a blanket against the night chill and went to take up her vigil.

The moon had grown one slice closer to full. Its thin light was watery, and the lantern's shifting glow denied it existed at all. Jamie sat down on the lid of the well and waited. Night cooled and thickened around her. She pulled the blanket around her shoulders. The night song of insects in the dry fields rose into a chorus. Her eyes grew heavy. Jami blew out her candle in the bedroom, completing the darkness. Outside the circle of her lamplight, creatures moved or perhaps her eyes played tricks on her. Her club rested across her lap. She tapped it with her fingernails, playing a rhythm. She knuckled her eyes and then vigorously scratched her head, trying to stay awake. She sang softly to herself, old songs. Wasn't there a third verse to that song? How had it begun?

She jolted awake.

She didn't remember reclining. The club that had been under her hand had been moved. Crouched at the edge of the well lid, staring at her with lambent green eyes, was the pecksie. One of her long-fingered hands rested on the club. Her silvery gray skin gleamed in the moonlight. "What do you do now?" the creature asked her.

Mirrifen sat up cautiously. She gathered her feet under her, ready to flee. "I'm guarding the well. The rats have been trying to gnaw through the cover. But if they do and fall in the well, they'll drown and foul the water."

"Not that!" the pecksie exclaimed with disdain. "You not guard. You sleep! But what you do now? You say, "Go away!" to pecksie? You send me to death?"

"No!" Mirrifen exclaimed in dismay. That part of Jami's story had horrified her. She shifted her weight and the pecksie backed to the edge of the lamplight, dragging the club with her. It was too big for her to wield; she was obviously taking it out of Mirrifen's reach. "I would never do that. Well, not unless you did something evil to me first."

"Pecksies don't kill babies."

"But they do eavesdrop."

The pecksie tilted her head at Mirrifen, frowning.

"Pecksies listen in when others are talking," Mirrifen clarified.

She shrugged one shoulder. "People talk and if pecksie is near, then a pecksie hears. And knows to be afraid."

"Well, you don't need to fear me. Not unless you do me an injury."

The pecksie frowned at her. "You gave me milk. I know I am bound."

"You said that. Not me. I didn't know that you would be bound by a simple favor. I didn't intend to do that."

"And this?" The pecksie held up her hand. Mirrifen's fever charm dangled from it. "Why you do this?"

It was Mirrifen's turn to shrug. "I saw you were hurt. Once I wanted to be a hedge-witch, to make charms like that. So I made one for you."

"Dangerous. It was wrong. I had to fix the beads. See. Yellow, then green." The pecksie tossed the little charm at her. By reflex, Mirrifen caught it. She studied it by lantern light and saw the change the pecksie had made.

"It was working when I left you."

"Worked. Just not as good as it could. Lucky for me, it not do harm. Hedge-witch has to be careful. Precise. Still. It worked. Worked better after I fix it."

Mirrifen examined the revised charm. "How did you know how to fix it?"

The pecksie folded her lips, then said briefly, "I know things. And again, I am bound."

"How do I unbind you?" Mirrifen asked.

The pecksie stared. When she decided she had understood Mirrifen's words, she spoke. "You can't. I took favor. I am bound."

"I didn't mean to bind you."

"I bound self when I took milk. Didn't have to. Could have died." Thoughtfully she rested a hand on her belly. Perhaps she thought of her unborn child.

"May I have my club back? In case rats come?"

"Rats already came."

"What?"

The pecksie gestured around at the darkness. Mirrifen lifted the lamp to expand the circle of light. She gasped.

Over a dozen dead rats littered the dusty ground around the well. Small arrows, no thicker than twigs, stood up from them. Pecksie hunters moved silently among them. Small black knives winked in the lantern's light as they skinned and butchered. "Good hunting here," the pecksie observed. "Last night, I scout. Tonight, we hunt. Better."

"Better for me, also." Mirrifen's eyes roamed the peculiar scene. She had not heard even a squeak during the slaughter. Even now, they butchered in silence. "They are so quiet."

"We are pecksies," the pecksie said with pride. "We hunt in dark, in silence. No words needed. Words are like coins. To spend carefully, as they are needed only. Not to scatter like humans do."

She looked aside and said carefully. "The rat blood is not enough. My folk need water."

"I will give you some. To thank you for guarding the well against the rats."

"We did not guard well. We hunted. I alone ask for water."

Mirrifen was unlatching the well hatch. "What about the others?"

"If you give water to me, I give to them," the pecksie admitted reluctantly.

Mirrifen had begun to lower the bucket into the well. When she heard the splash, she speculated aloud, "If I give water only to you, only you are bound. The others receive the water from you, not me."

"As you say," the pecksie grudgingly replied.

"So shall it be. I have no desire to bind pecksies." But even as she spoke, she wondered if she were foolish. If she withheld the water and forced them to beg for it, could she not bind all of them? And command all of them? They could do more than kill rats.

Or would they swarm her and take the water she taunted them with? Jami said they were vicious. She believed that pecksies had killed her mother.

She set the dripping bucket down before the pecksie. "I give this to you, pecksie."

"Thank you. I am bound," she replied formally. Then she turned to the rat butchers and twittered like a bat squeaking. They left off their butchering to mob the water. Some steadied the bucket while others hung head-down, drinking. And drinking. They emerged panting as if sating their thirsts had almost exhausted them. Mirrifen knew better than to offer to help. Instead she studied them. She imagined the long-fingered hands clutching at her, the sharp little teeth biting, dozens of them dragging her down. Yes. They could do that. Would they have? The pregnant pecksie presiding over the water didn't seem spiteful and vicious. But then, she was bound, and at Mirrifen's mercy. Perhaps she chose to present a fair face.

When the bucket was empty, it was smeared all over with silvery pecksie dust. The pecksie bowed and gravely asked, "May I have another bucket of water, mistress?"

"You may."

Mirrifen was still lowering the bucket when the pecksie spoke. "You thought about saying 'no' to me. To make all beg water and bind all to you. But you didn't. Why?"

Mirrifen presented the dripping bucket to the pecksie. She decided not to share all her thoughts. Counting her words like coins, she replied, "I've been bound that way. I promised to serve a hedge-witch in exchange for being taught the trade. I kept her house and tended her garden and even rubbed her smelly old feet. I kept my word but she didn't keep hers. I ended up half-taught, my years wasted. Such a binding breeds hate."

The pecksie nodded slowly. "A good answer." She cocked her head. "Then, you never command me?"

"I might," Mirrifen said slowly.

The pecksie narrowed her green eyes. "To what? To kill rats? To guard well?"

"You already kill rats. You will guard the well, because you want clean water. I don't need to command you to do that."

The pecksie nodded approvingly. "That is well said. No need to spend words to bind pecksie. So. You not bind pecksie?"

Mirrifen cleared her throat. Time to make Jami safe. "You must never harm Jami's baby." She recalled Jami's words, that pecksies counted words as precisely as a miser counted coins. This pecksie could still command other pecksies to do what she could not. She revised her dictum. "You must never allow harm to come to her baby."

The pecksie stared up at her. In the lamplight, her silvery face turned stony. "So. You bind me." She turned away from Mirrifen. She spoke to the night. "Almost I like you. Almost I think you are careful, deserve to be taught. But you believe stupid, cruel story. You throw words like stones. You insult pecksie. But I am bound. I obey. Not to harm the child, nor allow harm to come to it." The pecksie shook her head. "Careless words are dangerous. To all." She walked off. Mirrifen held up her lantern and watched her go. The hunters had all vanished, carrying their prey with them. Night was fading. The edge of an early summer dawn touched the horizon. Mirrifen went back to the farmhouse.

A few hours later, Mirrifen rose to do the morning chores. Jami slept on. There were fewer signs of rats in the house. Outside by the well, smudges of pecksie dust and smears of rat blood on the dry ground were the only signs of last night's visits.

She began to see signs of pecksies. The tracks of small bare feet on the dusty path. A smudge of silver near the cow's water bucket. A fall of dust made her glance up. A pecksie slept, careless as a cat, on the rafter of the cow's stall. Inside the chicken coop, she found all the hens alive and gathered half a dozen eggs. A silvery smear on one nesting box made her wonder if there had been seven eggs. When she spotted another pecksie sleeping soundly under the front steps, she hurried up them without stopping. The rats were gone, but now they were infested with pecksies. It unnerved her but it would do worse to Jami if she saw one.

Mirrifen scrambled eggs with milk and cut up the last of the week's bread. She had a steaming breakfast on the table when Jami emerged rubbing her eyes. She looked awful. Before Mirrifen could speak, she said, "I had nightmares all night. I dreamed pecksies stole my baby. I dreamed they'd attacked you by the well and killed you. I awoke near dawn, but I was too great a coward to get out of bed and see if you were all right. I just lay there, trembling and wondering if the pecksies would kill me next."

"I'm sorry you had such bad dreams. But as you see, I'm fine. Sit down and eat."

"I wish the men would come back. Drake would drive the pecksies away. I wish you'd had more hedge-witch training. Then you could make a charm to keep rats from the well and pecksies from the house."

Mirrifen bowed her head to that comment, trying not to feel rebuked. "I wish I knew how to make such charms. We'll just have to think of another way to deal with rats and pecksies."

Jami suggested fearfully, "Perhaps we could try my mother's trick. Leave food and water out for them, then bind them and send them away. They'd probably come for water."

"I don't think we need to do that, dear. I'll sleep beside you tonight, not out by the well."

"Why?"

Mirrifen gathered her courage. Yesterday, it had been hard to tell Jami that she must guard the well at night. It was even harder to tell her why she didn't need to do it anymore. She divulged the whole truth, of the injured pecksie and the binding with milk and finally of her command to the pecksie. Jamie flushed and then grew pale with fury.

"How could you?" she demanded when Mirrifen paused. "How could you bring a pecksie into this house after what I told you?"

"It was before you told me. I've made things right. I bound her not to do your baby any harm."

"You should send her away!" Jami's voice shook. "Withhold the water until they beg, then give it, bind them, and send them away! It's the only safe thing to do."

"I don't think that's right." Mirrifen tried to speak calmly. She and Jami seldom quarreled. "The pecksie doesn't seem dangerous to me. She seems, well, not that different from you and me, Jami. She's pregnant. I think she may be a pecksie hedge-witch. She said—"

"You promised Drake you'd take care of me. You promised! And now you're letting pecksies into the house. How could you be so false?" She leaped to her feet and rushed from the room, leaving her food half-eaten on the table. The bedroom door slammed. As she sighed in resignation, she heard a piercing shriek. The door was flung open so hard it bounded off the wall. Jami burst into the kitchen. "Pecksies! Pecksies were in my room last night! I didn't dream it, I didn't! Look, go and look!"

Mirrifen hurried to the bedroom and peered in. The room was empty. But on the floor in the corner, there was a bloody smudge by the silvery outlines of small feet. "It just killed a rat there," she said.

"And that? There?" Jami pointed accusingly at a smear of silvery tracks that ascended and crossed the bedclothes. Her finger swung again. "And there?" Silver smeared the windowsill. "What was it doing here? What did it want?" Jami's voice rose to the edge of hysteria. Mirrifen suspected that a pecksie had pursued a rat across the bed. She tried to sound comforting.

"I don't know. But I'll find out how they got in and block it off. And I won't sleep tonight. I'll keep watch over you."

The younger woman was torn between accepting her protection and displaying her anger at Mirrifen for bringing a pecksie into the house. Jami spent the rest of the day penduluming between the two reactions. Mirrifen devoted her hours to tightening the room against rats. In a corner, behind Jami's hope chest, the floor had sagged away from the wall, leaving a gap wide enough for a rat to slither through. The pecksie had obviously come through the open window. She found an old plank in the barn to mend the gap. As she came back to the house, she saw a pecksie clinging to the windowsill, peering into the bedroom. When she walked toward it, the pecksie sidled away quickly into the tall dry grass. The grasses didn't even sway after it.

That night, Mirrifen shut the door and the window tightly, and sat by the bed on a straight-backed chair. Long before midnight, her back and her head ached. She yawned and promised herself that tomorrow, after her chores, she'd take a long nap. A long nap, all by herself, stretched out in her own bed.

A tap on her knee woke her. She looked around at the darkness, momentarily bewildered. Pale moonlight cut between the thin curtains to slice the bed. Jami breathed evenly and deeply. Another tap on her knee brought her gaze down. The pecksie stood at her feet, looking up at her. Two more pecksies sat on the window sill. Three perched like birds on the footboard of the bed. All the pecksies stared at Jami intently. Mirrifen's pecksie spoke. "Mistress, may I have a bucket of water?"

The door to the room was still shut. "How did you get in here?" Mirrifen's voice shook slightly.

"By a way no rat could come. You bound me. 'Let no harm come to her child.' I must keep watch, to be sure it is so. These others serve me in that geas. Yours was the binding. How I fulfill it cannot concern you.

"Mistress, may I have a bucket of water?"

"I can keep watch over her myself," Mirrifen asserted shakily.

The pecksie shook her head sadly. "You spend your words in lies. You didn't guard. You slept. I am bound. Guard her I must."

Mirrifen rose stiffly from the chair. She crept from the room, the pecksie following. She motioned frantically for the others to follow but they did not take their gazes from Jami. She glanced at her pecksie beseechingly. The little woman shook her head stubbornly. "You spent the words, and this is what they bought you." Mirrifen felt like a traitor as she left Jami sleeping under the pecksies' watchful eyes. Her pecksie waited impatiently while she lit a lantern to give her courage.

Around the well, the silent slaughter of the night before had been repeated. The archers on the well cap were unstringing their bows as the butchers moved out to the skewered rats. It seemed to her that there were far more pecksies tonight. "Don't you fear that you'll run out of rats?" she asked.

"Drought will bring rats here. The well and your stored grain draw them." The pecksie gave her a sideways look. "But for us, rats would have eaten all grain. You should not be stingy if we take an egg sometimes."

Mirrifen bit back a retort and lifted the well hatch. The bucket's rope played out longer than it ever had. She said quietly, "If the drought lasts much longer, the well will go dry."

The pecksie didn't look at her. "You waste words on what you can't change."

Mirrifen drew the bucket up slowly. Every bucket of water she gave to the pecksie was one less bucket for Jamie and her. Mirrifen braced her courage and asked the question. "If I told you to leave our farm and take the other pecksies with you, you would have to do it."

The pecksie didn't answer the question. Instead she said, "You bound me to see that no harm comes to the child. To fulfill that, I must be where the child is." She stared off into the darkness. "Or the child must be where I am."

A chill went up Mirrifen's back. As she brought the brimming bucket to the surface, the pecksie said in a flat voice, "Thank you for the water, mistress. I am bound."

In less than a heartbeat, pecksies surrounded the bucket. The pecksie's fluting voice was stern, and they formed an orderly line. The water was rationed, each creature drinking for only a few seconds before another took his place. Nonetheless, Mirrifen drew four buckets of water before the horde was satisfied. The hatch thudded shut. The pecksie hunters dispersed. Her pecksie was the last to leave, walking not into the fields, but toward the house.

Slowly Mirrifen followed her. The house was silent. Inside the darkened bedroom, she sat down on the hard chair. She saw no pecksies, but knew they were there. The pecksie had said rats couldn't get into the room but there seemed no way to keep pecksies out.

She awakened late the next morning to Jami shaking her shoulder. "You slept! You promised to guard me, and then you slept!"

Sunlight flooded the room. The morning chores awaited and her head pounded from weariness. "I did my best. Please, Jami. Don't be angry. Nothing bad happened."

"Is this 'nothing bad'? What is this thing?"

Jami's thrust a hedge-witch charm at her. The amulet was smeared with silver but with a lurch of her heart, Mirrifen recognized beads and spindles from her own supplies. "I found it on top of me, right on my belly. The baby woke me, squirming inside me. He's never moved like that before!" She stared at Mirrifen and demanded, "Did you make this? What is it?"

Mirrifen shook her head as she reluctantly struggled to interpret the beads and knots. "It might be about something turning..."

"Oh, you don't know! It could mean anything! Anything!" Jami was trembling, her eyes welling tears. "Look around this room! Pecksie dust everywhere! They could have slit our throats as we slept."

"But they didn't. I bound her not to let harm come to your child. She can't hurt you without doing the child an injury. We've nothing to fear from them. Let me fetch some eggs for your breakfast. You'll feel better when you've eaten."

"I'll 'feel better' when you get rid of those pecksies. You know what you have to do, Mirrifen! Just do it! Why are you choosing them over me?"

If I sent her away, she'd have to take your baby with her. Mirrifen held the words back, unspent. She dared not reveal the double-edged geas she had put on the pecksie.

"I have to go let the chickens out."

As Mirrifen hurried from the room, Jami flung the charm after her. "You can't even say what kind of magic she did to me!" she shrieked.

As she fled to her chores, she saw signs of pecksies every-where. Footprints in the dust. Silver smears at the bottoms of the doors. Two thin pecksies were grubbing in the old kitchen gar-den. Her planted rows, shriveled as they were, remained intact. What were they finding in the untended part of the plot? Would they steal the little that remained of her garden?

One of the cows had gone dry and the other gave only a little milk. She gave each of the bony creatures a drink of water and turned them loose in the pasture. Two pecksies slept in the cows, empty manger. Two wakeful ones regarded her with fear-less agate eyes from the shade of the chicken house. The chicken house yielded four eggs, and two empty silvery shells, sucked dry. She crushed them and scattered it for the chickens to peck. She couldn't bear to tell Jami that the pecksies had taken the eggs, too. Why on earth had she helped the little creature?

The kitchen was mercifully free of rat droppings. At least the pecksies were doing some good. She heated water and wiped pecksie dust from the table and chairs. She thinned the milk with water and boiled oats in it and cooked the eggs in their shells. She set the meal out on the table and called Jami.

She didn't come.

She was sitting on the edge of the bed. Her hands were on her belly and her eyes were very big. "I think the baby wants to be born today," she said breathlessly. She bent over suddenly, gasping.

"I'll go for the midwife right away!"

"And leave me alone, at the mercy of your pecksies? No! No, you can't go! Mirrifen, you brought them here. If you won't send them away, at least stay and protect me."

There followed the longest day that Mirrifen had ever known. All morning, Jami labored unevenly. At noon, her pains eased, and she drowsed off. But the moment that Mirrifen rose, Jami roused. "Don't go! You can't leave me helpless here!"

"But, Jami, the midwife is—"

"Look! Look at them! They're just waiting for you to leave!" Jami's shaking hand pointed toward the window. As Mirrifen turned, the clustered pecksies on the outside sill leaped and fled. Silvery imprints where their faces had pressed the glass remained. Cold rose in Mirrifen's heart.

"I won't leave the house. I promise. I need some water from the kitchen."

The soft patter of fleeing feet preceded her down the hallway. Silvery handprints marred the walls. As she entered the kitchen, pecksies scattered into an open cupboard, behind the propped broom, and out the open door. Mirrifen snatched up the bucket and the dipper, slammed the door shut, seized the broom for a weapon, and then gasped to find no pecksie crouched behind it. She darted briefly into her own room. Her charm building supplies were scattered across her bed. She bundled them into her apron. Teeth gritted and arms laden, she hurried to Jami's bedroom and shut the door behind her. Jami had drowsed off again.

The pecksies had returned to their perch outside the window. Mirrifen shook her fist, and they fled like scalded cats. One remained, staring with jade eyes. "What you do?" the pecksie hedgewitch demanded as Mirrifen spilled her apron's contents the foot of Jami's bed. Mirrifen swished the thin curtains closed.

"I'll protect you," she promised the sleeping woman. With trembling hands, she sorted beads and spindles, rods for framework, various yarns and threads, and bits of feather and tufts of hair. She stole a glance at the pecksie crouched on the window sill, estimating her size and weight, memorizing the color of her eyes and hair. She didn't know the charm symbol for 'pecksie.' No matter. She knew 'person' and 'small' and the warding words that prevented creatures from passing through. Those would work well enough. She worked quickly but carefully, surprised at how her fingers remembered the correct knots and how to bind a feather in place. The finished charm was the size of a dinner plate. A final time she checked every knot, the placement of every bead. Yes. It would serve. She lifted it aloft as she spun to face the window, and was delighted to see dismay contort the pecksie's face. She squalled like a trodden-upon cat as she tumbled to the ground.

Mirrifen grinned, triumphant. She fastened the charm to the headboard of the Jami's bed.

Jami gave a sharp cry as a contraction jolted her from sleep. Mirrifen hastened to take her hands and gripped them firmly until the pain passed. "You'll be all right now," she assured Jami. "Look up. I've made a charm to keep pecksies from entering the room. You're safe now, dear."

"Oh, thank you," Jami whispered. Then she curled forward as her muscles tensed again. For two hours, her pains continued, growing in intensity and occurring closer together. "Soon now," Mirrifen kept telling her. "Soon your baby will be here." But contraction after contraction passed, and no child entered the world. Jami began to wail wordlessly with each pain; the sound set Mirrifen's teeth on edge.

As Jami panted between her pains, Mirrifen heard the scuff of small feet and a squeaking like bats outside the window. She kept the broom close to hand, in case the charm failed, but it held strong. No pecksie entered, though she heard their squeaking conversation outside. Slow hours passed, and Mirrifen held Jami's hands and told her that everything was fine.

Slowly she grew to know that she lied.

The long summer evening passed and the full moon that should have brought the baby shone through the curtain crack. Its light silhouetted crouched pecksies on the sill. Mirrifen ignored them. She gave Jami sips of water and wiped her sweating face. Jami's wails began to weaken with each succeeding pain.

Then, between Jami's moans, Mirrifen heard a scratching, as if a cat sought to enter. The pecksie spoke through the glass. "You must let us through," she said. There was an odd note to her words, beyond desperation. "You bind me two ways. Let us through. The child is in danger. Your charm is wrong! Open the way. Let us pass."

"No." Mirrifen spoke the word in a harsh whisper. *Go away.* Almost she spoke the words; she bit them back. She did not need to send the pecksie to her death. Her charm was keeping her at bay. Mirrifen fixed her eyes on Jami. The laboring woman was beyond caring for anything outside the limits of her own flesh. Mirrifen damped a corner of the bed sheet and wiped sweat from Jami's face. Her eyes were closed. She moaned softly, exhausted. Her belly rippled and then stilled. Jami drew a hoarse breath.

"Let me in." The pecksie's voice was louder. "You bound me. I must see that no harm comes to the child, but you will not let us through! She will die with the child inside her, and the child will die, too, if you do not let us through. You bound me. I cannot let him come to harm. Let us through."

"No!" And then, as the possible meaning of the words sank into Mirrifen's mind "NO!" she shouted. In a lower voice she added, "I will never let you in."

Jami stirred. She opened her eyes. "Water?" she begged.

"Not too much," Mirrifen cautioned, and held the dipper to her bitten lips.

She took a sip, and then gave a long caw of pain. When it passed, she whispered, "Oh, this can't be right. I've no strength left. The baby should be here by now."

"First babies always take a long time," she said, hating the lie. Jamie would die, painfully, the child dying within her.

"Help me," Jami said piteously.

"I don't know what to do," Mirrifen replied helplessly.

"Drake. Oh, Drake, I'm so sorry," Jami said. Her voice brimmed with sorrow, and resignation. "I'm so sorry, dear."

"You can't give up. You have to keep pushing, Jami. You have to."

"I can't," the young woman said quietly. "I can't." Her head lolled to one side and her eyes closed.

With a crash, glass shards scattered across the floor. The missile that had broken the window skidded to a stop by her foot. Mirrifen looked down. A charm. Familiar beads glittered alluringly on the framework. The web of threads drew her eyes into its wandering spiral that ended in a lock of dark hair. Her own, she knew. A sleep charm keyed to her. She could not look away. She fell to her knees beside Jami's bed, overcome by drowsiness. She pushed at the charm with a lax hand, trying to put it out of sight. Her fingers would not close to grip it. She managed to pull the edge of the blanket partially over it. It took all her will to look away from it.

On the window sill, pecksies crowded, poised to enter the room as soon as she slept. But her charm held them back, beyond the broken glass. Mirrifen's eyes sagged shut and her heavy head wobbled on her neck. She bit her lip hard and forced her eyes open. In that blink of darkness, a pecksie archer had appeared on the window sill. Slowly and steadily, he drew back his arrow and took careful aim at Jami.

"No!" she begged. "No! Please."

The arrow flew. Mirrifen heard the solid thud of its impact. A tiny rattling, of unstrung beads falling from a broken string, followed it. He'd shot, not Jami, but her warding charm. As its power failed, an avalanche of pecksies cascaded into the room, squeaking to one another. Mirrifen clutched at the blankets to stay upright. She had to protect Jami. She tried to grasp the sleep charm and throw it out the window. Her fingers wouldn't grip.

Then, hand over hand, the pecksie hedge-witch came up over the edge of Jami's bed. She carried a glittering black knife. In her other hand, she clutched the small charm that Jami had earlier discarded. She knelt between Jami's sprawled legs. She did not stir. Despite her terror, Mirrifen's eyes were closing. The pecksie met her gaze. There was no compassion there, no mercy at all. Only determination. "You bound me, and so I must do this. You charged me. 'Let no harm come to the child.' You chose this. " She set the charm on Jami's belly.

Then her long-fingered hand seized the fold of blanket and turned it back to bare the sleep charm. As Mirrifen sank to the floor, the pecksie said, "You should have spent your words more carefully."

꒰꒦꒱

Daylight washed through the shattered window and glittered on the broken glass on the silvery floor. Mirrifen blinked. She must have overslept. It was time to get up. Time to water the cows, time to feed the chickens. Time to make breakfast for Jami…

"Jami!" Mirrifen sat bolt upright.

The pecksie sitting on Jami's bed opened her small hand. A cascade of charm beads fell from it, to rattle and roll on the floor. She flicked away the lock of Mirrifen's hair.

"What did you do? Oh, what did I do?" Even with the charm destroyed, she felt she was surfacing from deep black water. Everything seemed too bright.

A very pale Jami lay still on the bed. A baby, firmly swaddled, rested against her side. The baby's eyes were closed, but as Mirrifen watched, his lips puckered, pursed for a moment and then relaxed. "Oh, Jami," Mirrifen sighed in sorrow. Then her heart leapt as Jami's lids fluttered and opened. She smiled weakly at Mirrifen.

"He's just like his father. All he wants to do is eat."

"That's good. That's so good," Mirrifen managed to say. Jami's eyes were already sagging shut. Even her lips were pale.

"She will live."

Mirrifen startled at the pecksie's voice. "Thank you," she said faintly. Groggily she got to her feet. She looked questioningly at the pecksie.

"You believe stupid stories. 'Pecksies kill babies.' Ha! This pecksie save her baby. Save her, too." The little woman gave Mirrifen a dark look. "And not just because you say, 'no harm to child,' and dead mother is harm to child. I save because pecksies not filthy, wicked things. Now you go milk cow, get eggs, cook. She needs food, rich food. So does pecksie."

As Mirrifen walked toward the kitchen, the pecksie waddled along at her side. "What did you do?" Mirrifen asked.

"Broke your stupid 'no pass' charm that kept baby inside her. Turned baby. Cut mother, just a little. Helped baby out."

"Cut her." Mirrifen shivered. "Will she be all right?"

"Sore. Weak. Better than dead. Feed her, rest her. She be better. She already less stupid."

"Less stupid?"

"Knows pecksies saved her. Saved baby." The little woman shrugged. "Less stupid about pecksies."

"Thank you." Mirrifen met the pecksie's eyes. "I'm sorry I bound you. I'd undo it if I could."

"I took milk." The pecksie shrugged. "Bound myself." She sat down on the kitchen floor with a sigh. "And you?" the pecksie asked her. "Are you less stupid?"

"It was my fault, wasn't it? When I made a charm that said small people could not pass, I kept the baby from being born. I should have been more careful."

The pecksie nodded grimly. "You less stupid now." She cocked her head at Mirrifen. "Do chores. I stay here."

Mirrifen paused at the door. "You're a hedge-witch, aren't you?"

The pecksie considered it. "Stupid words. Pecksie not a hedge, not a witch. Pecksie a charm-maker."

She could not bring herself to ask. "I always wanted to be a charm-maker."

The pecksie narrowed her green eyes. "Will you bind me to teach you?"

Mirrifen shook her head. "No. Never again. Words are too dangerous to bind anyone with them."

"I teach, then." A small smile of approval bent her cat's mouth. "You learning already."